HOME on the RANCH

SHIPMENT 5

The Texan's Baby by Donna Alward
Not Just a Cowboy by Caro Carson
Cowboy in the Making by Julie Benson
The Renegade Rancher by Angi Morgan
A Family for Tyler by Angel Smits
The Prodigal Cowboy by Kathleen Eagle

SHIPMENT 6

The Rodeo Man's Daughter by Barbara White Daille
His Texas Wildflower by Stella Bagwell
The Cowboy SEAL by Laura Marie Altom
Montana Sheriff by Marie Ferrarella
A Ranch to Keep by Claire McEwen
A Cowboy's Pride by Pamela Britton
Cowboy Under Siege by Gail Barrett

SHIPMENT 7

Reuniting with the Rancher by Rachel Lee
Rodeo Dreams by Sarah M. Anderson
Beau: Cowboy Protector by Marin Thomas
Texas Stakeout by Virna DePaul
Big City Cowboy by Julie Benson
Remember Me, Cowboy by C.J. Carmichael

SHIPMENT 8

Roping the Rancher by Julie Benson
In a Cowboy's Arms by Rebecca Winters
How to Lasso a Cowboy by Christine Wenger
Betting on the Cowboy by Kathleen O'Brien
Her Cowboy's Christmas Wish by Cathy McDavid
A Kiss on Crimson Ranch by Michelle Major

HOME *on the* RANCH

COWBOY
FOR HIRE

———— ⚒ ————

USA TODAY BESTSELLING AUTHOR

MARIE
FERRARELLA

Recycling programs
for this product may
not exist in your area.

ISBN-13: 978-1-335-45297-9

Cowboy for Hire

Printed in U.S.A.

 HARLEQUIN®
www.Harlequin.com

To
Dianne Moggy,
for being nice enough
to call and reassure me.
Thank you.

Prologue

There had to be more.

There just had to be more to life than this.

The haunting thought echoed over and over again in Constance Carmichael's brain as she sat in her father's dining room, moving bits and pieces of chicken marsala around on her plate.

Her father was talking. But not to her—or even *at* her, as was his custom. This time his words were directed to someone on the other end of his state-of-the-art smartphone. From what she had pieced together, someone from one of his endless construction projects. Carmichael Construction Corporation, domiciled in Houston, Texas, had projects in different stages of completion throughout the country, and Calvin Carmichael thrived on the challenge of riding roughshod on *all* of his foremen.

The table in the dining room easily sat twenty. More if necessary. Tonight it only sat two, her father and her. She was here by mandate. Not that she didn't love her father, she did, but she had never been able to find a way to bond with him—not that she hadn't spent her whole life trying. But she had never been able to approach him and have him see her as something other than the ongoing disappointment he always made her feel that she was.

Calvin Carmichael didn't believe in pulling any punches.

Rather than sharing a warm family dinner, Connie had rarely felt more alone. She felt utterly isolated—and distance was only part of the reason. Before the call came in, her father had insisted that she sit at one end of the table while he sat at the other.

"Like civilized people," he'd told her.

He was at the head of the table and consequently, she was at the foot—with what felt like miles of distance between them.

If merely sharing a meal had been her father's main objective, it could have been more easily attained than this elaborate command performance. Connie was aware of restaurants that were smaller than her father's dining room. She'd grown up in this enormous house, but it had never felt like home to her.

She watched Fleming, her father's butler, retreat out of the corner of her eye. It was no secret that Calvin Carmichael enjoyed with relish all the perks that his acquired wealth could buy, including not just a cook and a housekeeper but a genuine English butler, as well. The latter's duties included serving dinner, even if the only one at the table was her father.

Connie sighed inwardly, wondering when she could safely take her leave. She knew that if her sigh was audible, her father would make note of it. Moreover, he'd grill her about it once his phone call was over, finding a way to make her feel guilty even if he was the one at fault.

Sitting here, toying with her food and watching her father, Connie felt a numbing malaise, a deadness spreading like insidious mold inside her. Surrounded by wealth, able to purchase and own any object her heart desired, no matter how extravagant, she found she desired nothing.

Because nothing made her happy.

She knew what she needed.

She needed to feel alive, to feel productive. She needed to accomplish something so that she could feel as if she finally, finally had a little of her father's respect instead of always being on the receiving end of his thinly veiled contempt.

"You're not eating. I invited you for dinner, you're not eating. Something wrong with your dinner?"

Connie looked up, startled. Her father had been on the phone for the past twenty minutes, but the slight shift in his tone made her realize that he had ended his conversation and had decided to find some reason to criticize her.

Connie lifted her shoulders in a careless, vague shrug. "I'm just not hungry, I guess," she replied, not wanting to get into an argument with the man.

But it seemed unavoidable.

"That's because you've never *been* hungry. Had you grown up hungry," Calvin stressed, "you would never waste even a *morsel* of food." Crystal-blue eyes narrowed beneath imposing, startlingly black eyebrows. "What's wrong with you, little girl?" If the question was motivated by concern, there was no indication in either his inflection or his tone.

Little girl.

She was twenty-seven years old, and she *hated* when her father called her that, but she knew it was futile to say as much. Calvin Carmichael did what he pleased *when* he pleased to whomever he pleased and took no advice, no criticism from anyone. To render any would just get her further embroiled in a heated exchange. Silence usually won out by default.

"Haven't I given you everything?" Calvin pressed, still scowling at his only daughter. His only child according to him. He had long since disowned the older brother she had adored because Conrad had deigned to turn his back on the family business and had struck out on his own years ago.

Connie looked at her father for a long moment. This feeling wasn't about to go away, and if she didn't say anything, she knew it would only get worse, not to mention that her father wouldn't stop questioning her, wouldn't stop verbally poking at her until she told him what he claimed he wanted to know.

As if he cared.

"I don't want to be *given* anything," she told her father. "I want to *earn* it myself."

His laugh was belittling. "Earn it, right. Where's this going, little girl?"

She pressed her lips together for a moment to keep from saying something one of them—possibly both of them—would regret. Her father didn't respond well to displays of emotion.

"I want to helm a project." It wasn't really what was bothering her, but maybe, just maybe, it might help squash these all but paralyzing doldrums that had infiltrated her very soul.

"You? Helm a project?" Piercing blue eyes stared at her in disbelief. "You mean by yourself?"

She tried not to react to the sarcasm in her father's voice. "Yes. My own project."

He waved a dismissive hand at her. "You don't know the first thing about being in charge of a project."

Anger rose within her, and she clutched to it. At least she was finally *feeling* something. "Dad, I've worked for you in one capacity or another for the last ten years. I think I know the first thing about being in charge of a project—and the second thing, too," she added, struggling to rein in her temper. An outburst would only tilt the scales further against her.

Her father was a formidable man, a man who could stare down his opponents and have them backing off, but she was determined not to allow him to intimidate her. She was fighting for her life—figuratively and, just possibly, literally.

Calvin laughed shortly. But just before he began to say something scathing in reply, his ever-present cell phone rang again.

To Connie's utter annoyance, her father answered it. It was time to leave, she decided. This "discussion," like all the others she'd had with him over the years, wasn't going anywhere.

But as she pushed her chair back and rose to her feet, Connie saw her father raise a finger, the gesture meant to keep her where she stood.

"Just a minute."

She wasn't sure if he was speaking to her or the person on the other end of the call. His next words, however, were definitely directed at her.

"Forever." For a moment, the word just hung there, like a single leaf drifting down from a tree. "Let's see what you can do about getting a project up, going and completed in Forever."

Something in her gut warned her she was walking into a trap—but she had no other choice. She had to do it—whatever "it" turned out to be.

"What kind of a project?" she asked warily.

Her father's attention already appeared to be elsewhere. "I'll have Emerson give you the particulars," he said in an offhanded manner, referring to his business manager. "Just remember, little girl, I started with nothing—I don't intend to wind up that way," he warned her, as if he was already predicting the cost of her failure.

Adrenaline was beginning to surface, whether in anticipation of this mysterious project or as a reaction to her father's condescending manner, it was hard for her to tell—but at least it was there, and she was grateful for that.

"Thank you," she said.

But her father was back talking to the person on the other end of the cell phone, giving that man his undivided attention.

She had a project, Connie thought, savoring the idea as it began to sink in. The world suddenly got a whole lot brighter.

Chapter One

"I can't believe what you've done to the place," Brett Murphy said to Finn, the older of his two younger brothers, as he looked around at what had been, until recently, a crumbling, weather-beaten and termite-riddled ranch house.

This morning, before opening up Murphy's, Forever's one and only saloon, he'd decided to look in on Finn's progress renovating the ranch house he had inherited from one of the town's diehard bachelors. And though he hadn't been prepared to, he was impressed by what he saw.

"More than that," Brett added as he turned

to face his brother, "I can't believe that you're the one who's doing it."

Finn never missed a beat. He still had a lot to do before he packed it in for the day. "And what's that supposed to mean?" he asked. He'd been at this from first light, wrestling with a particularly uncooperative floorboard trim, which was just warped enough to give him trouble. That did *not* put the normally mild-tempered middle brother in the best frame of mind. "I built you a bathroom out of practically nothing, didn't I?" he reminded Brett. The bathroom had been added to make the single room above the saloon more livable. Until then, anyone staying in the room had had to go downstairs to answer nature's call or take a shower.

Brett's memory needed no prodding. It had always been a notch above excellent, which was fortunate for his brothers. It was Brett who took over running Murphy's and being financially responsible for them at the age of eighteen.

"Yes, you did," Brett replied. "But don't forget, you were the kid who always wound up smashing his thumb with a hammer practically every time you so much as held one in your hand."

His back to Brett as he continued working, Finn shrugged. "You're exaggerating, and anyway, I was six."

"I'm not—and you were twelve," Brett countered. He inclined his head ever so slightly as if that would underscore his point. "I'm the one with a head for details and numbers."

Finn snorted. It wasn't that he took offense, just that their relationship was such that they took jabs at one another—and Liam—as a matter of course. It was just the way things were. But at bottom, he was fiercely loyal to his brothers—as they were to him.

"Just because you can add two and two doesn't make you the last authority on things, Brett," Finn informed his brother.

"No, running Murphy's into the black pretty much did that."

When, at eighteen, he had suddenly found himself in charge of the establishment, after their uncle Patrick had died, he'd discovered that the saloon was actually *losing* money rather than earning it. He swiftly got to work making things right and within eight months, he'd managed to turn things around. It wasn't just his pride that was at stake, he had brothers to support and send to school.

"Look, I didn't swing by to squabble with you," Brett went on. "I just wanted to see how the place was coming along—and it looks like you're finally in the home stretch. Liam been helping you?" he asked, curious.

This time Finn did stop what he was doing. He looked at Brett incredulously and then laughed. "Liam? In case you haven't noticed, that's a box of tools by your foot, not a box of guitar picks."

Finn's meaning was clear. Of late, their younger brother only cared for all things musical. Brett still managed to get Liam to work the bar certain nights, but it was clear that Liam preferred performing at Murphy's rather than tending to the customers and their thirst.

"I thought Liam said he was coming by the other day," Brett recalled.

"He did." Finn's mouth curved. "Said watching me work inspired his songwriting."

"Did it?" Brett asked, amused.

Finn shrugged again. "All I know was that he scribbled some things down, said 'thanks' and took off again. I figure that *he* figures he's got a good thing going. Tells you he's coming out here to help me then when he comes here, he writes his songs—and calls it working." There was no resentment in Finn's voice as he summarized his younger brother's revised work ethic. For the most part, Finn preferred working alone. It gave him the freedom to try different things without someone else second-guessing him or giving so-called advice. "Hey, Brett?"

Brett had wandered over to the fireplace. Finn had almost completely rebuilt it, replacing the old red bricks with white ones. It made the room look larger. "What?"

"You think our baby brother has any talent?" he asked in between hammering a section of the floorboard into place.

"For avoiding work?" Brett guessed. "Absolutely."

Finn knew that Brett knew what he was referring to, but he clarified his question, anyway. "No, I mean for those songs he writes."

Brett could see the merit in Liam's efforts, especially since he wouldn't have been able to come up with the songs himself, but he was curious to hear what Finn's opinion was. Since he was asking, Brett figured his brother had to have formed his own take on the subject.

"You've heard him just like I have," Brett pointed out, waiting.

Finn glanced at him over his shoulder. "Yeah, but I want to know what you think."

Brett played the line out a little further. "Suddenly I'm an authority?" he questioned.

Down on his knees, Finn rocked back on his heels, the frustrating length of floorboard temporarily forgotten. Despite the fancy verbal footwork, he really did value Brett's take on things. Brett had been the one he'd looked up to when he was growing up.

"No, not an authority," Finn replied, "but you know what you like."

"I think he's good. But I think he's better at singing songs than he is at writing them," he said honestly, then in the next moment, he added, "But what I *do* know is that you've got a real talent for taking sow's ears and making silk purses out of them."

Never one to reach for fancy words when plain ones would do, Finn eyed him with more than a trace of confusion.

"How's that again?" he asked.

Brett rephrased his comment. Easygoing though he was, it wasn't often that he complimented either of his brothers. He'd wanted them to grow up struggling to always reach higher rather than expecting things to be handed to them—automatic approval readily fell into that category.

"You're damn good at this remodeling thing that you do."

Finn smiled to himself. Only a hint of it was evident on his lips. "Glad you like it."

"But you don't have to work on it 24/7," Brett pointed out. Finn had immersed himself in this huge project he'd taken on almost single-handedly. There was no reason to push himself this hard. "Nobody's waving a deadline at you."

"There's a deadline," Finn contradicted. He saw Brett raise an eyebrow in a silent query, so he stated the obvious. "You and Lady Doc are still getting married, aren't you?"

Just the mere mention of his pending nuptials brought a wide smile to Brett's lips. Just the way that thoughts of Alisha always did.

Until the young general surgeon had come to town, answering Dr. Daniel Davenport's letter requesting help, Brett had been relatively certain that while he loved all the ladies, regardless of "type," there was no so-called soul mate out there for him.

Now he knew better, because he had met her. Not only was she out there, but he would be marrying her before the year was out, as well.

"Yes," Brett replied. "But what...?"

Finn anticipated Brett's question and cut him short. "This is my wedding present to you and Lady Doc—to say thanks for all the times you were there for Liam and me when we needed you—and even the times when we thought we didn't," he added with a touch of whimsy. "And this is, in a small way, to pay you back for staying instead of taking off with Laura right after high school graduation, the way she wanted you to.

"In other words, this is to say thanks for staying, for giving up your dream and taking care of your two bratty younger brothers instead."

While Finn and Liam were aware of Laura, he had never told them about the ultimatum she'd given him. Had never mentioned how tempted he'd been, just for a moment, to follow her to Los Angeles. All his brothers knew was one day, Laura stopped coming around.

He looked at Finn in surprise. "You know about that?"

Finn smiled. "I'm not quite the oblivious person you thought I was."

"I didn't think you were *oblivious*," Brett corrected him. "It was just that you saw and paid attention to things the rest of us just glossed over." His smile widened as he looked around the living room. Finn had outdone himself. "But seriously, this is all more than terrific, but this is *our* ranch house," he emphasized, "not just mine."

Finn looked at him and shook his head in wonder before getting back to work. "You bring that pretty Lady Doc here after you've married her and she finds out that she's sharing the place with not just you but also your two brothers, I guarantee that she'll walk out of here so fast, your head'll spin clean off."

He might not be as experienced as Brett was when it came to the fairer sex, Finn thought, but some things were just a given.

"Now, I don't know nearly as much as you do when it comes to the ladies, but I do know that newlyweds like their own space—that doesn't mean sharing that space with two other people. Liam and I'll go on living at the house. This'll be your place," he concluded, waving his hand around the room they were currently in as well as indicating the rest of the house.

"But the ranch itself is still *ours,* not just mine," Brett insisted.

"Earl Robertson left it to you," Finn stated simply. The man, he knew, had done it to show his gratitude because Brett had gone out of his way to look in on him when he had taken sick. That was Brett, Finn thought, putting himself out with no thought of any sort of compensation coming his way for his actions.

"And I've always shared whatever I had with you and Liam," Brett stated flatly.

Finn allowed a sly smile to feather over his lips, even though being sly was out of keeping with his normally genial nature.

"I see. Does that go for Lady Doc, too?"

Brett knew that his brother was kidding and that he didn't have to say it, but he played along, anyway. "Alisha is off-limits."

Finn pretended to sigh. "It figures. First nice *thing* you have in eons, and you're keeping it all to yourself."

"Damn right I am."

Finn changed the subject, directing the conversation toward something serious. "Hey, made a decision about who your best man is going to be?"

Brett was silent for a moment. He'd made Finn think he was debating his choices, but the truth of it was, he'd made up his mind from the beginning. It had been Finn all along.

"Well, Liam made it clear that he and that band of his are providing the music, so I guess you get to be best man."

His back to Brett, Finn smiled to himself. "I won't let it go to my head."

"Might get lonely up there if it did," Brett commented with affection. He glanced at his watch. "Guess I'd better be getting back or Nathan McHale is going to think I've abandoned him," he said, referring to one of the two most steadfast patrons at Murphy's.

Finn laughed. "Wonder how long he'd stand in front of the closed door, waiting for you to open up before he'd finally give up."

Brett began to answer without hesitation. "Two, maybe three—"

"Hours?" Finn asked, amused.

"Days," Brett corrected with a laugh. The older man had been coming to Murphy's for as many years as anyone could remember, motivated partially by his fondness for beer and most assuredly by his desire to get away from his eternally nagging wife, Henrietta. "I'll see you later tonight."

Finn nodded. "I'll be by when I get done for the day," he said. He was back to communing with another ornery section of floorboard before his brother walked out the front door.

Connie had decided to just drive around both through Forever and its surrounding area to get a general feel for the little town. For the most part, it appeared she'd stumbled across a town that time had more or less left alone. Nothing looked ancient, exactly, and there were parking places in front of the handful of businesses rather than hitching posts, but all in all, the entire town had a very rural air about it, right down to the single restaurant—if a diner could actually lay claim to that title.

She'd been amused to see that the town's one bar—how did these cowboys survive with only one bar?—had a sign in the window that said "Hungry? Go visit Miss Joan's diner. Thirsty? You've come to the right place." That had told her that there was obviously a division of labor here with territories being defined in the simplest of terms.

Given its size and what she took to be the residents' mind-set, Connie doubted very much if a place like this actually *needed* a hotel—which, she had a feeling, had probably been her father's whole point when he had given her this *project,* saying if she wanted to prove herself to him, he wanted to see her complete the hotel, bringing it in on time and under budget. The budget left very little wiggle room.

"Newsflash, Dad. I don't give up that easily," she murmured to the man who was currently five hundred miles away.

Challenges, especially seemingly impossible ones, were what made her come alive. At first glance, the sleepy little town of Forever needed a hotel about as much as it needed an expert on wombats.

It took closer examination to see that the idea of building a hotel had merit.

Connie could see the potential of the place forming itself in her mind's eye. She just needed the right approach, the right thing to play up and the hotel-to-be would not only become a reality, it would also be a success and eventually get its patrons.

But it wouldn't get anything if it wasn't first built, and she had already decided that while she could have materials shipped in from anywhere in the country that could give her the best deal, to get the structure actually built, she was going to use local *talent,* so to speak.

She naturally assumed that living out here in what she viewed as *the sticks* made people handy out of necessity. Unlike in the larger cities, there wasn't a range of construction companies, all in competition with one another, all vying for the customer's money.

Driving down here from Houston, she had already ascertained that the nearest town, Pine Ridge, was a minimum of fifty miles away. That alone limited the amount of choices available. If anything, out here it was the unhandy customer who wound up searching to find someone to do the work for them.

Just like faith, the right amount of money, she had learned, could move mountains.

She had no mountains to move. But she did have a building to erect, and in order not to be the outsider, the person who was viewed as invading their territory, she would need allies. In this particular case, she needed to have some of the men from Forever taking part in making the hotel a reality.

Granted that, once completed, the hotel would belong to the Carmichael Construction Corporation until such time as they sold it, but she had to make the locals feel that building the hotel would benefit the whole town as well as provide them with good-paying jobs during construction.

Connie knew the importance of friends; she just didn't exactly know how to go about making them.

But she had done her homework before

ever getting behind the wheel of her vehicle and driving down here.

As she drove around now, Connie thought about the fact that on the other side of the town, located about ten miles due north-west, was a Native American reservation. She couldn't remember which of the tribes lived there, but perhaps they would welcome the work, along with Forever townspeople. Given the local state of affairs, who wouldn't want a job?

So, armed with her GPS, Connie was on her way there. She was driving slower than she was accustomed to for two reasons: one, she didn't have a natural sense of direction, and she didn't know the lay of the land, and, two, she wanted and *needed* to get to know this land she was temporarily camping out on.

The reservation was her destination, but something—instincts perhaps—made her closely scan the immediate area she was tra-versing.

Which was when she saw him.

At first she thought she was having a hallu-cination, a better-than-average morning fan-tasy that could easily trigger her latent libido if she let it. The trick to being a driven woman with not just goals, but also the taste of success tucked firmly under her belt, was the way she responded to things that needed life-long commitments. It required—demanded, really—tunnel vision. Eye on the prize and all that sort of thing.

Even so, Connie slowed her pristine, gleaming white BMW sports car down to an arthritic crawl as she stared at the lone figure in the distance.

No harm in just looking, she told herself.

Even at this distance, she could easily make out that the man was around her own age. She was keenly aware that he was bare-chested, that his muscles were rippling with every move he made and that, pound for pound, he had to be the best-looking specimen of man-hood she had seen in a very long time.

Moving closer, she could see that perspiration covered his body, causing practically a sheen over his chest and arms.

At first she wasn't aware of it, but then she realized that her mouth had gone bone-dry. She went on watching.

He didn't seem to be aware of the fact that he was under scrutiny. The worker turned his back to her and went on doing whatever it was that he was doing. She couldn't quite make it out, but it had something to do with construction because there were tools on the ground, surrounding an empty tool chest.

As she continued observing him, Connie saw that the man appeared as if he not only knew his way around tools, but he also definitely seemed comfortable working with his hands.

It came to her then.

He was just the man she was looking for to be her foreman, to act as her go-between with whatever men she wound up hiring to do the actual work. Watching him, she couldn't help wondering how well someone who looked like that would take instructions from a woman.

Or was he the type who didn't care who issued the orders as long as there was a guaranteed paycheck at the end of the week?

Enough thinking, start doing, she silently ordered herself.

The next moment, she turned her vehicle toward the cowboy and drove straight toward him.

Chapter Two

He'd been aware of the slow-moving, blindingly white sports car for some time now. It was a beauty—much like the woman who was driving it.

But unlike the woman behind the wheel, the vehicle, *because* of its make and model, stuck out like a sore thumb. Regardless of the season, Forever and its outlining area didn't see much through traffic. Every so often, there was the occasional lost traveler, but on the whole, that was a rare occurrence. Forever was *not* on the beaten path to anywhere of interest, except perhaps for the reservation and a couple of other tiny towns that had sprung up in the area. On its way to being a ghost town more than once, the town stubbornly survived despite all odds. Like a prickly pear cactus, Forever, a few of the much older residents maintained, was just too ornery to die.

The owner of the sports car, Finn decided, had to be lost. Nobody driving that sort of a vehicle could possibly have any business being in or around Forever. Even Dan, the doctor who had initially come to town out of a sense of obligation mixed with a heavy dose of guilt, hadn't been driving a car nearly that flashy and unsuitable for this terrain when he'd arrived.

As the vehicle came closer, Finn tossed down his hammer and approached the car. The woman, he couldn't help noticing, was even better-looking close up than she was at a distance.

"You lost?" he asked her, fully expecting her to sigh with relief and answer "Yes."

She didn't.

Instead, she shook her head and said, "No, I don't think so."

Finn regarded her thoughtfully. "In my experience, a person's either lost or they're not. There is no gray area."

The woman smiled at him. "Didn't think I'd find a philosopher all the way out here."

"It's not philosophy, it's just plain common sense," Finn told her.

To him, so-called *philosophers* referred to the gaggle of retired old men who got together every morning and sat on the sun-bleached bench in front of the general store, watching the rest of the town go through its paces and commenting on life when the spirit moved them. He was far too busy to indulge in that sort of thing.

"Well, if you don't need directions, then I'll get back to my work," he told her. The woman was clearly out of her element, but if she didn't want to talk about what she was doing out here, he wasn't about to prod her. Lost or not, it was strictly her business.

"I don't need directions, but I do have a question." She raised her voice as if to get his attention before he began hammering again.

Finn turned back to face her. She looked rather fair. He could see a sunburn in her near future if she didn't at least put the top up on her car. Skin that fair was ripe for burning.

"Which is?" he asked casually.

"Did you build this yourself?" The woman

got out of her car and crossed to the freshly rebuilt front steps of the house.

Thanks to Brett, honesty had always been at the core of his behavior. His older brother expected and accepted nothing less than that. Anyone can lie, Brett maintained, but it took a real man to tell the truth each and every time, even when it wasn't easy.

"No," Finn replied. "The ranch house was already here. I just changed things around a little, replaced what needed replacing, added a little here, a little there—that kind of thing," he told her simply.

He made it sound as if he'd hammered down a few loose boards, but one look at the exterior told her that the man with the impossibly appealing physique had done a great deal more than just that. The structure looked brand-new. She knew for a fact that this part of the state was hard on its buildings and its terrain. Summers could be brutal, and they left their mark on practically everything, especially structures. The ranch house she was looking at had been resurfaced, replaced and renovated—and recently.

Connie couldn't help wondering if that craftsmanship extended to the inside of the building, as well.

There was only one way to find out.

"Could you take me on a tour of the inside of the house?" she asked brightly.

"I could," the cowboy answered but made no effort to follow through on her request.

"But?" she asked.

She made him think of a stick of dynamite about to go off. He was about ten inches taller than she was, but a stick of dynamite didn't have to be very big to make a sizable impression.

Just who was this woman, and what was she doing here? "But I don't even know who you are."

"I'm not dangerous, if that's what you're thinking," she told him.

Like he believed that.

Finn's mouth curved ever so slightly, the left side more than the right. He wondered just how many men this woman had brought to their knees with that killer smile of hers.

"There's dangerous, and then there's *dangerous*," he replied, his eyes never leaving hers.

She raised her chin just a little, doing her best to generate an air of innocence as she assured him, "I'm neither."

The cowboy continued looking at her.

The image of a human lie detector flashed through her mind for an instant. She discovered that breathing took a bit of concentration on her part.

"I don't know about that," he said. But the next moment, he seemed to shrug away his assessment of her and said, "Okay, why not? Don't lean against anything," he warned before going up the porch steps. "The paint's still fresh in places."

She had no intentions of taking away any part of this house on her person. "I'll keep that in mind," she told him.

Connie waited for her tour guide to open the front door. If the inside looked nearly as good as the outside, she was ready to be blown away.

"After you," the cowboy told her once he'd opened the front door.

Connie crossed the threshold, taking it all in at once.

She hadn't missed her guess. The inside of the house was simplistic and all the more captivating for that. It was a house that emphasized all things Western, with just the right touch of modern thrown in to keep the decor from being completely entrenched in the past.

There were only a few pieces of furniture.

For the most part, the house was empty, but then, she hadn't asked to come in just to see the furniture. She was looking to take stock of the workmanship firsthand.

She hadn't been wrong.

This cowboy did have a gift for bringing things together—and apparently, a knack for knowing just when to back off.

"How long have you been working on this?" she asked, wanting as much input from the man and *about* the man as she could get.

"Awhile," Finn replied vaguely, as if wondering just what her end game was.

While this woman had apparently been taking stock of the house as he went about showing her around the two floors, Finn did the same with her. So far, he hadn't come to any useful conclusion. She hadn't really volunteered anything except a few flattering comments about his work. He still had no idea what had brought her to Forever, or even if she *meant* to come to Forever, or was just passing by on her way to somewhere else.

"Awhile," the woman repeated, going back to what he'd said about his timetable. "Does that mean six months or six years or what?"

"Awhile means awhile," he replied in a

calm voice, then added, "I'm not exactly keeping a diary on this."

"Then you're just doing this for fun?"

"Not exactly." Because he could see that she intended to stand there, waiting, until he gave her some sort of a more satisfying answer, he told her. He saw no reason not to. "It's a wedding present."

"For your bride?" she guessed.

Finn nearly choked. He didn't intend to get married for a very long time. Possibly never.

"No," he denied with feeling. "For my brother. It's *his* wedding."

"And this is his house?" she asked, turning slowly around, this time taking in a three-hundred-sixty-degree view. No doubt about it, she thought. The work done on the ranch house was magnificent.

"He says it belongs to all three of us, but Earl Robertson's will left it to him." And as far as he and Liam were concerned, this was Brett's house.

"Honor among brothers. That's refreshing."

He thought that was an odd way to phrase it. "Don't know one way or the other about *refreshing*. Do know what's right, though, and this house is right for Brett and Lady Doc."

"Lady Doc?" she repeated, slightly confused.

"That was the nickname my brother gave Alisha when she first came to Forever. Alisha's a doctor," he told her by way of a footnote. "Look, lady, I'd love to stand around and talk some more—it's not every day that we see a new face around here—but I really do have to get back to work."

The woman raised her hands in mock surrender, showing the cowboy that she was backing off and giving him back his space. "Sorry. I didn't mean to take you away from your work."

Having said that, she turned on her heel and headed back to her vehicle.

As he watched her walk away, Finn found himself captivated by the way the woman's hips swayed with every step she took. It also occurred to him at the same time that he didn't even know her name.

"Hey," he called out.

Ordinarily, that was *not* a term Connie would answer to. But this one time, she made an exception. People acted differently out here. So rather than get into her car, Connie turned around and looked at him, waiting for the cowboy to say something further.

Raising his voice, Finn remained where he was. "You got a name?" he asked.

"Yes, I do," Connie replied.

With that she slid in behind the steering wheel of her car, shut her door and started up her engine.

Always leave them wanting more was an old adage she had picked up along the way, thanks to her grandfather. Her grandfather had taught her a great many things. He had told her, just before he passed away, that he had great faith in her. The only thing her father had ever conveyed to her was that she was a huge and ongoing source of disappointment to him.

Her grandfather, she knew, would have walked away from her father a long time ago. At the very least, he would have given up trying to please her father, given up trying to get him to take some sort of positive notice of her.

But she was too stubborn to give up.

Knocked down a number of times for one reason or another, she still got up, still dusted herself off and was still damn determined to someday make her father actually pay her a compliment—or die trying to get it out of him.

Connie spent the rest of the afternoon driving around, getting marginally acquainted with the lay of the surrounding land. She took in the reservation, as well—if driving around its perimeter could be considered taking it in. She never got out of her vehicle, never drove through the actual terrain because even circumnavigating it managed to create an almost overwhelming sadness within her.

Her father had been right about one thing. She was a child of affluence. The sight of poverty always upset her. But rather than fleeing and putting it out of her mind, what she had seen seemed to seep into her very soul. She could not imagine how people managed to go on day after day in such oppressive surroundings.

It also made her wonder why the reservation residents didn't just band together, tear some of the worst buildings down and start fresh, putting up something new in their place.

Not your problem, Con. Your father issued you a challenge. One he seemed pretty confident would make you fall flat on your face. It's up to you to show him once and for all that he's wrong about you. That he's underestimated you all along.

That thought was still replaying itself in her head when she finally drove back into

Forever late that afternoon. She was hungry, and the idea of dinner—even one prepared at what she viewed to be a greasy-spoon establishment—was beginning to tempt her.

But as much as she wanted to eat, she wanted to finish up her homework even more.

In this case, her homework entailed checking out the local—and lone—bar to see the kind of people who hung out there. She wanted to meet them, mingle with them and get to know them, at least in some cursory fashion. She was going to need bodies if she hoped to get her project under way, and Murphy's was where she hoped to find at least some of them.

Right now all she knew was that her father had purchased a tract of land within Forever at a bargain price because no one else was interested in doing anything with it. A little research on her part had shown that the town was deficient in several key departments, not the least of which was that it had nowhere to put up the occasional out-of-town visitor—which she just assumed Forever had to have at least once in a while. That particular discovery was confirmed when she went to book a hotel room and found that the nearest hotel was some fifty miles away from the center of Forever.

The hick town, her father had informed her through Emerson, his right-hand man, needed to have a hotel built in its midst. Giving her the assignment, her father washed his hands of it, leaving all the details up to her.

And just like that, it became her responsibility to get the hotel built for what, on paper, amounted to a song.

Her father had hinted that if she could bring the project in on time and on budget—or better yet, *under* budget, he might just take her potential within the company more seriously.

But she needed to prove herself worthy of his regard, of his trust. And until that actually happened, he had no real use for her. He made no effort to hide the fact that he was on the verge of telling her that he no longer needed her services.

Connie had every intention of showing her father just what a vital asset she could be to his construction conglomerate. She also promised herself that she was going to make him eat his words; it was just a matter of time.

Stopping her vehicle behind Murphy's, Connie parked the car as close to the building as she could. The gleaming white sports car wasn't a rental she was driving, it was her own car. She wasn't superstitious by nature, but every good thing that had ever happened to her had happened when she was somewhere within the vicinity of the white sports car. It was, in effect, her good-luck talisman. And, as the embodiment of her good fortune, she wanted to keep it within her line of vision, ensuring that nothing could happen to it.

She intended on keeping an eye on it from inside the bar.

However, Connie quickly discovered that was an impossibility. For one thing, the bar's windows didn't face the rear lot.

Uneasy, she thought about reparking her car or coming back to Murphy's later, after dinner.

But then she reminded herself that her car had a tracking chip embedded within the steering wheel. If her car was stolen, the police could easily lay hands on it within the hour.

Provided they knew about tracking chips and how to use them, she qualified silently. She took measure of the occupants within the bar as she walked in. The first thought that crossed her mind was that the people around

her could never be mistaken for the partici-
pants in a think tank.

Still looking around, she made her way to
the bar, intending on ordering a single-malt
beer.

A deep male voice asked her, "What'll it
be?" when she reached the bar and slid onto
a stool.

The voice sounded vaguely familiar, but
she shrugged the thought away. She didn't
know anyone here. "What kind of beer do
you have on tap?" she asked, continuing to
take inventory of the room.

"Good beer."

The answer had her looking at the bartender instead of the bar's patrons. When she
did, her mouth dropped open.

"You," she said in stunned surprise.

"You," Finn echoed, careful to hide his initial surprise at seeing her.

Unlike the woman seated at that bar, he'd
had a couple of minutes to work through his
surprise. It had spiked when he first saw
her walk across the threshold. Disbelief had
turned into mild surprise as he watched her
make her way across the floor, weaving in
and out between his regular patrons.

When she'd left the ranch this morning,

he'd had a vague premonition that he would be seeing her again—but he hadn't thought that it would be this soon. He should have known better. The woman had asked too many questions for someone who was just passing through on her way to somewhere else.

"So what are you?" The woman posed the question to him. "A rancher or a bartender?"

"Both," he said without the slightest bit of hesitation. Around here, a man had to wear a lot of hats if he planned on surviving. "At least, that's what my brother says."

"The one who's getting married," she recalled.

So, she had been listening. That made her a rare woman, Finn concluded. The women in his sphere of acquaintance talked, but rarely listened. "That's the one."

"You have any more brothers?"

"Yeah, he's a spare in case I wear the other one out."

The woman looked around, taking in the people on either side of her. The bar had its share of patrons, but it was far from standing-room only. Still, there were enough customers currently present—mostly male—for her to make a judgment.

"Something tells me that the men around here don't wear out easily."

"You up for testing that theory of yours out, little lady?" Kyle Masterson proposed, giving her a very thorough once-over as he sidled up to her, deliberately blocking her access to the front door.

Chapter Three

Although he remained behind the bar, Finn's presence seemed to separate the talkative cowboy from the young woman who had wandered onto Brett's ranch earlier. Finn was 85 percent certain that Kyle, a rugged, rather worn ranch hand, was harmless. But he was taking no chances in case Kyle was inspired by this woman and was tossing caution to the wind.

"Back to your corner, Masterson," Finn told him without cracking a smile. "The lady's not going to be testing out anything with you to-night."

Kyle, apparently, had other ideas. "Why

don't you let her speak for herself, Murphy?" the other man proposed. "How about it, little lady?" he asked, completely ignoring Finn and moving in closer to the woman who had caught his fancy. "We could take us a stroll around the lake, maybe look up at the stars. See what happens."

His leer told her exactly what the hulking man thought was going to happen. Amused, Connie played out the line a little further. "And if nothing happens?" she posed.

"Then I will be one deeply disappointed man," Kyle told her, dramatically placing a paw of a hand over his chest. "C'mon, little lady. You don't want to be breaking my heart now, do you?" He eyed her hopefully, rather confident in the outcome of this scenario he was playing out.

"Better that than me breaking your arm, Masterson," Finn informed him, pushing his arm and hand between them as he deliberately wiped down the bar directly in the middle.

Kyle glanced from Finn to the very appealing woman with hair the color of a setting sun. It was obvious he was weighing his options. Women came and went, but there was only one saloon in the area. Being barred from Murphy's was too high a price to pay for a fleeting flirtation.

"Oh, is it like that, now?" the cowboy guessed.

"Like what?" Connie looked at the man, not sure she understood his meaning.

Amazingly deep-set eyes darted from her to the bartender and then back again, like black marbles in a bowl.

Kyle grinned at the bartender. "Don't think I really have to explain that," he concluded. Raising his glass, he toasted Finn. "Nice work, laddie." And with that, the bear of a man retreated into the crowd.

Brett approached from the far side of the bar. "Problem?" he asked, looking from his brother to the very attractive young woman at the bar. He'd taken note of the way some of his patrons were watching her, as if she were a tasty morsel and they were coming off a seven-day fast in the desert. That spelled trouble—unless it was averted quickly.

"No, no problem," Finn replied tersely. As grateful as he was to Brett and as much as he loved and respected him, he hated feeling that his older brother was looking over his shoulder. He wasn't twelve anymore, and hadn't been for quite some time. "Everything's fine."

"That all depends," Connie said, contradicting Finn's response. She had a different take on things, one that had nothing to do with the hulking cowboy and his unsuccessful advances.

Brett looked at her with interest. "On?"

"On how many men I can get to sign on with me," Connie replied.

The sudden, almost syncopated shift of bodies, all in her direction, plainly testified that the exchange between the young woman and two of the saloon's owners was far from private. Leers instantly materialized, and interweaving voices were volunteering to sign on with her no matter what the cause.

In Finn's estimation, it was obvious what the men's leers indicated that they *believed* they were signing up for—and tool belts had nothing to do with it.

To keep the crowd from getting rowdy and out of control, Finn quickly asked the question, "Sign on to what end?" before Brett could.

Crystal-blue eyes swept over the sea of faces, taking preliminary measure of the men in the saloon. "I need a crew of able-bodied men to help me build a hotel," she answered.

"Build a hotel?" an older man in the back

echoed incredulously. By the way he repeated the proposed endeavor, it was obvious that a hotel was the last structure he would have thought the town needed. He wasn't alone. "Where you putting a hotel?"

Connie answered as if she was fielding legitimate questions at a business meeting. "The deed says it's to be constructed on the east end of town, just beyond the general store."

"Deed? What deed?" someone else within the swelling throng crowing around her asked.

Connie addressed that question, too, as if it had everything riding on it. She had learned how *not* to treat men by observing her father. He treated the men around him as if they were morons—until they proved otherwise. She did the exact opposite.

Employees—and potential employees—had her respect until they did something to lose it.

"The deed that my company purchased a little less than three weeks ago," she replied, then waited for the next question.

"Deeds are for ranches," Nathan McHale, the most steadfast and longest-attending patron of Murphy's, said into his beer, "not hunks of this town."

Connie shifted her stool to get a better look at the man. "I'm afraid you're wrong there, Mr.—?" She left the name open, waiting for the man to fill it in for her.

Nathan paused to take a long sip from his glass, as if that would enable him to remember the answer to the newcomer's question. Swallowing, he looked up, a somewhat silly smile on his wide, round face.

"McHale."

"Don't worry about him, missy. Ol' Nathan's used to being wrong. The second he steps into his house, his wife starts telling him he's wrong," Alan Dunn, one of the older men at the far end of the bar, chuckled.

Nathan seemed to take no offense. Instead, what he did take was another longer, more fortifying drink from his glass, this time managing to drain it. Putting the glass down on the bar, he pushed it over toward the bartender—the younger of the two behind the bar.

Connie noticed that the latter eyed his customer for a moment, as if deciding whether or not to cut the man off yet. She knew that she definitely would—and was rather surprised when the bartender decided not to.

For all his girth and folds, McHale looked

like a child at Christmas, his eyes lighting up and a wreath of smiles taking over his rounded face. He gave the bartender who had refilled his glass a little salute as well as widening his appreciative smile.

Using both hands, he drew the glass to him, careful not to spill a single drop. Then, just before he took his first sip of his new drink, McHale raised it ever so slightly in a symbolic toast to the newcomer. "You were saying?"

"I was saying—" Connie picked up the thread of her conversation where it had temporarily stopped "—that my construction company has purchased the deed for a section of the town's land."

"You here to see if the town wants to buy it back?" Brett asked, curious.

There'd been complaints from time to time that there was nowhere to stay if anyone was stranded in Forever overnight. But things always got sorted out for the best. The sheriff enjoyed telling people that was how he and his wife, Olivia, had first gotten together. On her way to track down her runaway sister, Olivia'd had no intentions of staying in Forever. Her car had had other ideas. She'd wound up relying on the hospitality of the town's resident wise woman and diner owner, Miss Joan.

"No," Connie replied patiently, "I'm here to build a hotel."

"A hotel?" It was someone else's turn to question the wisdom of that. Obviously, more than one person found this to be an odd undertaking. "What for?" the person asked.

"For people to stay in, you nitwit," the man sitting on the next stool informed him, coupling the sentence with a jab in the ribs.

"What people?" a third man asked. "Everyone around here's got a home."

Connie was ready for that, as well. She'd read up on Forever before ever setting out to see it. She knew her father wouldn't have given her an easy project. That had never been his way.

"Well, if there's a hotel here," she said, addressing her answer to the entire bar, "it might encourage people to come to Forever."

"Why would we want people to come here?" the man who'd asked her the question queried again. "We got all the people we know what to do with now."

Several other voices melded together, agreeing with him.

Connie was far from put off, but before she

could say anything, the good-looking man she'd seen this afternoon beat her to it.

"She's talking about the town growing, Clyde," Finn pointed out. "You know, *progress*."

Connie fairly beamed at the bartender, relieved that at least *someone* understood what she was trying to convey. "Exactly," she cried.

"Hell, progress is highly overrated," Clyde declared sourly. He downed his shot of whiskey, waited for it to settle in, then said, "I like this town just fine the way it is. Peaceful," he pronounced with a nod of his bald head.

This was not the time or the place to become embroiled in a hard sell. The land officially now belonged to her father's company, thanks to some negotiations she had not been privy to. That meant that the decision as to what to do or not do with it was not up to the people lining the bar.

Be that as it may, she was still going to need them, or at least some of them, to help with the hotel's construction. That meant she couldn't afford to alienate *any* of them. Besides the fact that local labor was always less expensive than bringing construction workers in, hiring locals always built goodwill. There wasn't a town or city in the country that hadn't felt the bite of cutbacks and didn't welcome an opportunity to obtain gainful employment, even on a temporary basis.

This was not the first project she was associated with, although it was the first that she was allowed to helm on her own. She already knew she was going to need a few skilled workers, like someone who could handle the backhoe, and those people would be flown in. But as for the rest of it, the brawn and grunt part, those positions she hoped she would be able to fill with people from in and around the town. The one thing she knew she could count on was that extra money was always welcomed.

Connie raised her voice, addressing Clyde. "I promise not to disturb the peace." For good measure, she elaborately crossed her heart. "I came here to offer you jobs. I need manpower to help me make this hotel a reality."

This time it was Kyle Masterson who spoke up. He hired out to some of the local ranchers, but he had never been afraid of hard work. "What kind of money we talking about?"

She made eye contact with the big man. "Good money," she responded in all seriousness.

"How much?" Brett asked, trying to pin

her down not for himself, but for the men who frequented Murphy's, men he knew were struggling with hard times and bills that were stamped *past due*.

"Depends on the level of skills you bring to the job," she replied honestly. "That'll be decided on an individual basis."

"Who's gonna do the deciding?" another man at the bar asked.

The question came from behind her. Connie turned to face whoever had spoken up. They were going to find out sooner or later, might as well be sooner, she thought. "I am."

"Big decisions," the man responded with a laugh. He eyed her in clear amusement. She obviously looked like a slip of a thing in comparison to the men she was addressing. "You sure you're up to it, honey?"

Connie had never had any slack cut for her. Her father had made sure that she was treated like a crew member no matter what job she was doing. The fact that she was willing to— and did—work hard had not failed to impress the men, even if it seemed to have no effect whatsoever on her father.

Connie looked the man asking the question directly in the eye and said with no hesitation, "I am. Are you?"

Her answer generated laughter from the other men around the bar.

"She's got you there, Roy. Looks like you better make nice if you want to earn a little extra for your pocket," the man next to him advised.

"It'll be more than just a *little extra*," Connie was quick to correct. "And if you work hard and get this project in on time and on budget, everyone on the project will get a bonus."

The promise of a bonus, even an unspecified one, never failed to stir up positive goodwill, and this time was no exception. Snippets of responses and more questions furiously flew through the air.

"Sounds good!"

"Count me in."

"Hey, is the bonus gonna be as big as the salary?"

"You calculating that by the hour or by the day?"

Finn had stood by, holding his tongue for the most part. The woman doing the talking had intrigued him right from the start when she'd first approached him this morning. Since his bent was toward building, anyway, he figured that he might have to do a little negotiation with Brett to get some free time in order to get involved on this construction project.

But he didn't see that as being a problem. Brett was fairly reasonable when it came to things like this. He'd given Liam a lot of slack so he could practice and rehearse with his band. As far as older brothers went, a man would have to go to great lengths to find someone who was anywhere near as good as Brett.

"Looks like you've got them all fired up and excited," Finn commented to the young woman as he checked her glass to see if she needed a refill yet.

"How about you? Do I have you all fired up and excited?" she asked, going with his wording. Connie shifted the stool to face him. The man was still her first choice to head up the work crew. The other men might be good—or even more capable—but so far this so-called bartender's handiwork had been the only one she'd seen firsthand.

But the moment she phrased the question, she saw her mistake.

Finn had every intention of giving her a flippant answer, but there was something in her eyes, something that had him skidding to a grinding halt and reassessing not just his answer, but a hell of a lot of other things, as well. Things that had nothing to do with tools and construction.

The woman on the stool before him probably had no idea that she had the kind of eyes that seemed to peer into a man's soul while making him reevaluate everything that had happened in his life up to this singular moment in time.

A beat went by before he realized that she was still waiting for him to respond.

"Yes," he answered quietly, his eyes on hers. He found he couldn't look away even if he wanted to—which he didn't. "You do," he added in the same quiet tone.

Despite the surrounding din, his voice managed to undulate along her skin and lodge itself directly beneath it.

It took Connie more than a full second to come to, then another full second to find her voice and another one after that to realize that her mouth and throat had gone bone-dry. If she said more than a couple of words, they could come out in a comical croak, thereby negating whatever serious, or semiserious, thing she was about to say.

Taking the drink that was on the bar before her, she emptied the glass in an effort to restore her voice to its initial working order. Tears suddenly gathered in her eyes as flames coasted through her veins. She'd forgotten her glass contained whiskey, not something less potent.

"Good," she managed to say without the word sticking to the roof of her mouth. Taking a breath, she willed herself to be steady and then completed her sentence. Nothing could interfere with work. She wouldn't allow it to. "Because I have just the position for you."

Most likely not the same position I have in mind for you.

The thought, materializing out of nowhere, took Finn completely by surprise. He was extremely grateful that the words hadn't come out of his mouth. It wasn't his intention to embarrass either himself or the young woman.

But he found that he was having trouble banishing the thought out of his head. The image seemed to be all but burned into his brain. An image that was suddenly making him feel exceedingly warm.

Finn focused on the hotel she had been talking about. This represented the first move toward progress that had been made in Forever in quite some time.

"What kind of a position?" he asked her out loud, rubbing perhaps a bit too hard at a spot on the bar's counter.

"Is there someplace we can talk?" she asked him.

Finn thought of the room that was just above the saloon. Initially, their uncle Patrick had lived there when he'd owned and operated Murphy's. On his passing, it had been just an extra room that all three of them had sporadically availed themselves of if the occasion warranted it. Currently, however, Brett's fiancée was staying there, but only when she wasn't working—or staying with Brett at the ranch. The clinic was still open, which meant that the room would be empty.

But Finn didn't feel comfortable just commandeering it—besides, Brett would undoubtedly have his head if he found out.

The next moment, Finn felt he had come up with a viable alternative. "Have you had dinner yet?" he asked the woman.

"No." She had been so worked up about this project, so eager to get it going, that she had completely forgotten about eating.

"Then I know just the place we can talk. Brett," Finn called, turning toward his brother. "I'm taking my break now."

Motivated by his interest in anything that had an effect on the town, Brett had discreetly listened in on the conversation between Finn and this woman. He appeared mildly amused at his brother's choice of words. "You planning on being back in fifteen minutes?"

"A couple of breaks, then—plus my dinner break," Finn added for good measure.

"You already took that, don't you remember?" Brett deadpanned.

"Then my breakfast break," Finn shot back, exasperated.

Brett inclined his head. "That should work," he told Finn. "Just don't forget to come back," he called after his brother as Finn made his way around the bar.

Escorting the woman through the throng of patrons, most of whom were now keenly interested in what this newcomer to their town had to offer, Finn waved a hand over his head. This signified to Brett that he had heard him and was going to comply—eventually.

"Where are we going?" Connie asked once they made it through the front door.

"To dinner," Finn repeated.

"And that would be—?"

Finn grinned. "At Miss Joan's," he answered.

"Miss Joan's?" she repeated. The name meant nothing to her.

"The diner," Finn prompted. "It's the only restaurant in town."

For now, Connie corrected silently. Plans for the hotel included a restaurant on the premises.

But for the time being, she thought it best to keep that to herself.

Chapter Four

Since she had already ascertained that it was the only so-called restaurant in town, Connie had initially intended on checking the diner out after she left Murphy's. But seeing the cowboy who had, she admitted—although strictly to herself—taken her breath away—both because of his craftsmanship *and* his physique—she'd temporarily lost sight of the plan she'd laid out for herself to round out her first day in Forever.

The bartending cowboy opened the door for her and she stepped into the diner. Connie scanned the area, only to discover that everyone in the diner was looking right back at her.

Before taking another step, she unconsciously squared her shoulders.

Inside the brash, confident young woman who faced down all sorts of obstacles, beat the heart of a shy, young girl, the one whose father had always made her feel, through his words and through his actions, that she wasn't good enough. That she couldn't seem to measure up to the standards he had set down before her.

Even though he had told her, time and again, that she was a source of constant disappointment to him, Calvin Carmichael had insisted that, from the relatively young age of fourteen, his only daughter replace her late mother and act as a hostess at the parties that he threw for his business associates.

It was while acting as hostess at those very same parties that she developed her polish and her poise—at least on the surface. Only her father knew how to chip away at that veneer to get to the frightened little girl who existed just beneath that carefully crafted surface.

To be fair, her father had been just as demanding of her brother, Conrad. But Conrad had been far more rebellious than she ever was. He absolutely refused to be bullied and left home for parts unknown the moment that he turned eighteen.

She would have given *anything* to go with him, but she was only fourteen at the time, and Conrad had enough to do, looking after himself. He couldn't take on the burden of being responsible for a child, as well.

At least that was what she had told herself when he'd left without her.

So Connie resigned herself to remaining in her father's world, desperately treading water, determined to survive as best she could. Not only surviving, but vowing to one day make her father realize how wrong he'd been about her all along. It was the one thing that had kept her going all this time.

The *only* thing.

Was it her imagination, or were the occupants of the diner looking at her as if she were some sort of an unknown entity?

She inclined her head in her companion's direction, lowering her voice to a whisper. "You weren't kidding about not many tourists passing through this town. These people really aren't used to seeing strangers walking their streets, are they?"

Finn's mouth curved ever so slightly. "Forever's not exactly on the beaten path to anywhere," he pointed out. Although, even if Forever was a regular bustling hotbed of activity, he could see this woman still turning heads wherever she went.

"That's becoming pretty clear," Connie whispered to him.

"Been wondering when you'd finally step in here," the thin, older woman with the somewhat overly vibrant red hair said as she sidled up to the couple to greet them. "What'll it be for you and your friend here, Finn?" she asked, nodding her head toward the other woman. "Table or counter?"

Connie was about to answer "Counter," but the man the hostess had referred to as "Finn" answered the question first.

"Table."

The woman nodded. "Table it is. You're in luck. We've got one table left right over here." So saying, the redhead led them over to a table near the kitchen. There was only one problem, as Connie saw it. There was a man still sitting at it.

Connie regarded the other woman. "But it's occupied," she protested. Did the woman think they were going to join the man?

The woman appeared unfazed. "Hal here finished his dinner," she explained, indicating the table's lone occupant. "He's just a might slow in getting to his feet, aren't you, Hal?" she said, giving her customer exactly ten seconds of her attention. Then she looked around for the closest waitress and summoned her. "Dora." She beckoned the young blonde over. "Clear the table for Finn and his friend, please." She offered the couple just a hint of a smile. "I'll be back to get your orders in a few minutes. Sit, take a load off," she encouraged, patting Connie on the shoulder. And then she added, "Relax," and turned the single word into a strict command.

Dora was quick to pick up and clear away the empty dinner plate from the table. Within two minutes, Dora retreated, and Connie realized that she and the cowboy were left alone with their menus.

Connie was only mildly interested in glancing over the menu and that was purely out of a curiosity about the locals' eating preferences. As always, eating, for Connie, took a backseat to orientation.

She decided to begin with the very basics. Names. Specially, his name. "That woman, the one with the red hair, she called you Finn."

"That's because she knows my name," he

replied simply. Finn had a question of his own to ask her. "But I don't know yours."

"I didn't tell you?" The omission on her part surprised her. She'd gotten so caught up in getting her operation set up and hopefully rolling soon in this tiny postage-stamp-size town that common, everyday details had slipped her mind.

"You didn't tell me," Finn confirmed, then added with yet another, even more appealing hint of a smile, "I'm not old enough to be forgetful yet."

Not by a long shot, Connie caught herself thinking. Just for a moment, she got lost in the man's warm, incredibly inviting smile.

Get back on track, Con. Drooling over the employees isn't going to get this project done—and it just might mess everything all up.

One way or another, she'd been lobbying her father for a chance to show her stuff for a while. Now that she finally had it, she was *not* about to allow something as unpredictable as hormones to betray her.

"My name is Constance Carmichael," she told him, putting out her hand.

"Nice to meet you, Ms. Carmichael." Her hand felt soft, almost delicate in his, he couldn't help thinking. His hand all but swallowed hers up. "I'm Finn Murphy."

"Like the bar?" she asked, trying to fit two more pieces together.

"Like the bar," he confirmed.

"My father's Calvin Carmichael," Connie added.

She was accustomed to seeing instant recognition whenever she mentioned her father's name. The second she did, a light would come into people's eyes.

There was no such light in the bartending cowboy's eyes. It prompted her to say, "He founded Carmichael Construction Corporation."

Still nothing.

Finn lifted his broad shoulders in a self-deprecating shrug and apologized. "Sorry, 'fraid it doesn't ring a bell for me."

That was when it hit her. "I guess it wouldn't," Connie said. "The corporation only erects buildings in the larger cities." The moment she said it, she knew she had made a tactical mistake. The man sitting across the table from her might take her words to be insulting. "I mean—"

Finn raised his hand to stop whatever she might be about to say. "Forever *is* small," he assured her. "And that leads me to my question for you."

Her eyes never left his. "Go ahead."

Having given him the green light, Connie braced herself for whatever was going to be coming her way. Something told her that Finn was one of the key players she would need to solidly win over and keep on her side if she hoped to not only get this project under way, but completed, as well.

"If your dad's company just builds things in big cities, then what are you doing scouting around someplace like Forever?" It didn't make any sense to him. He loved the place, but there wasn't anything exceptional about Forever to make outsiders suddenly sit up and take notice.

It's personal, Connie thought, silently answering him.

Granted, the man was pretty close to what one of her friends would have termed *drop-dead gorgeous,* but she didn't know a single thing about him other than he was good with his hands and could tend bar, so trusting him with any part of her actual life story would have been beyond foolish, beyond reckless and definitely stupid.

Connie searched around for something

neutral to say that would satisfy Finn's curiosity. And then she came up with the perfect response.

"He's branching out," she told him, then fell back on what had always been a surefire tactic: flattery. "Besides, there's a lot of potential in little towns like yours."

Though he wasn't quite sold, Finn quietly listened to what this stunningly attractive woman had to say. For now, he'd allow her to think he'd accepted her flimsy explanation. Since she was obviously sticking around, he figured that eventually, he'd find out just what part of what she had said was the truth.

Miss Joan picked that moment to all but materialize out of nowhere, a well-worn pad held poised in her hand. "So, you two ready to order yet?" she asked them.

Finn had barely glanced at the menu, but then, he didn't really have to. His favorite meal was a permanent fixture on the second page.

"I am," he told Miss Joan, "but I don't think that Ms. Carmichael's had a chance to look at the menu just yet."

Rather than go with the excuse that Finn had just provided her with, Connie placed her menu on top of his and told the woman, "I'll just have whatever he's having."

"How do you know it's any good?" Finn challenged, mildly surprised by her choice. "Or that you'll like it?"

"I'm a quick judge of character, and you wouldn't order anything that was too filling, or bad for you. You told your brother that you were coming back to work the rest of your shift. That means that you can't be too full or you'll get drowsy," she concluded. "Besides, I'm not very fussy."

Miss Joan smiled in approval, then nodded toward her as she said to Finn, "This one's smart. Might want to keep her hanging around for a bit. Okay, boy," Miss Joan said, shifting gears when she saw the slight change of color in Finn's complexion, "what'll it be?"

Finn placed his order, asking for a no-frills burger and a small order of home fries, along with some iced coffee. Miss Joan duly noted his order, then murmured, "Times two," before she glanced over toward Finn's companion. She waited for the young woman to change her mind.

She didn't.

About to leave, Miss Joan turned abruptly

and looked at Finn's tablemate. "Ms. Carmichael," she repeated thoughtfully.

"Yes?" Connie considered the older woman, not quite knowing what to expect.

The light of recognition came into Miss Joan's sharp, amber eyes. "Your daddy wouldn't be Calvin C. Carmichael now, would he?"

"You know my father?"

She would have expected the bartender and the people around his age to know who her father was. Since he apparently didn't, she felt it was a given that someone around this woman's age—someone she assumed had been born here and most likely would die here—would have never even *heard* of her father.

"Mostly by reputation," Miss Joan admitted. She thought back for a moment. "Although I did meet the man once a long time ago. He was just starting out then," she recalled. And then her smile broadened. "He was a pistol, all right. Confident as all getout, wasn't about to let anything or anyone stop him." Miss Joan nodded to herself as more facts came back to her. "He was bound and determined to build himself an empire. From what I hear now and again, he did pretty much that."

Rather than wait for any sort of a comment or a confirmation from Finn's companion, Miss Joan asked another question, a fond smile curving her mouth. "How's your mother doing?"

"She died a little over twelve years ago," Connie answered without missing a single beat, without indicating that the unexpected reference to her mother felt as if she had just been shot point-blank in her chest. Twelve years, and the wound was still fresh.

Usually, she had some sort of an inkling, a forewarning that the conversation was going to turn toward a question about or a reference to her mother. In that case, Connie was able to properly brace herself for the sharp slash of pain that always accompanied any mention of her mother. But this had been like a shot in the dark, catching her completely off guard and totally unprepared and unprotected.

Sympathy flowed through Miss Joan and instantly transformed and softened the woman's features.

"Oh, I'm so sorry to hear that, dear." She placed a comforting hand on the younger woman's shoulder. "As I recall, she was a lovely, lovely woman. A real lady," she added with genuine feeling. Dropping her hand, Miss Joan began to withdraw. "I'll get that order for you now," she promised as she took her leave.

The woman sitting opposite him appeared to be trying very hard to shut down, Finn thought. He was more than familiar with that sort of reflexive action, building up high walls so that any pain attached to the loss was minimized—or as diminished as it could be, given the circumstances.

"I'm sorry about that," Finn said to her the moment they were alone again. "Miss Joan doesn't mean to come on as if she's prying. Most of the time, she just has a knack for getting to the heart of things," he told her gently.

"Nothing to apologize for," Connie answered, shaking off both his words and the feeling the older woman's question had generated. "The woman—Miss Joan, is it?" she asked. When Finn nodded, Connie went on. "Miss Joan was just making idle conversation."

Her mouth curved just a little as she allowed herself a bittersweet moment to remember. But remembering details, at times, was becoming harder and harder to do.

"She actually said something very sweet about my mother. At this point, it's been so long since she's been gone that there are times

I feel as if I just imagined her, that I never had a mother at all." She shrugged somewhat self-consciously. She'd said too much. "It's rather nice to hear someone talk about her, remember her in the same light that I do."

Because his heart was going out to her, Finn had this sudden desire to make her realize that she wasn't the only one who had suffered this sort of numbing loss so early in her life.

"I lost my mother when I was a kid, too. Both my parents, actually," Finn amended.

Despite his laid-back attitude about life and his easygoing manner, to this day it still hurt to talk about his parents' deaths. One moment they had been in his life, the next, they weren't. It was enough to shake a person clear down to their very core.

"Car accident," he said, annotating the story. "My uncle Patrick took my brothers and me in." A look Connie couldn't fathom crossed his face. The next moment, she understood why. "A few years later, Uncle Patrick died, too."

Completely captivated by his narrative, she waited for Finn to continue. When he didn't, she asked, "Who took care of you and your brothers after that? Or were you old enough to be on your own?"

"I was fourteen," he said, answering her question in his own way. "Brett had just graduated from high school. He was turning eighteen the following week, so he petitioned to be officially declared our guardian."

What he had only recently discovered was that his brother had done that at great personal sacrifice—the girl Brett loved was setting out for the west coast. She'd asked Brett to come with her. Given a choice between following his heart and living up to his responsibility, his older brother had chosen responsibility—and never said a word about it.

"I guess you might say that Brett actually raised Liam and me—it just became official that year," Finn concluded fondly.

He and Brett had their occasional differences, but there was no way he could ever repay his brother for what Brett had done for him as well as Liam.

Connie laughed shortly. "When I was fourteen, my brother took off." She said the words dismissively, giving no indication how hurt she'd been when Conrad left her behind.

"College?" Finn guessed.

She actually had no idea where her brother

went or what he did once he left her life. She hadn't heard from him in all these years.

"Maybe." She thought that over for a second. It didn't feel right to her. Conrad had been neither studious nor patient. "Although I doubt it. My father wanted my brother to go to college, and Conrad wanted to do whatever my father didn't want him to do."

"Is that why you're working for Carmichael Construction?" he asked. "Because your father wants you to?"

Remembering the look on her father's face when they had struck this deal, Connie laughed at the suggestion. Having her as anything but a lowly underling in the company was *not* on her father's agenda. The man was not pushing her in an attempt to groom her for bigger, better things. He was pushing her because he wanted to get her to finally give up and settle into the role of family hostess permanently.

"Actually," she replied crisply, "my father doesn't think I have anything to offer the company. I'm working at the corporation because *I* want to," Connie emphasized.

Reevaluating the situation, Finn read between the lines. And then smiled. "Out to prove that he's wrong, is that it?"

It startled her that he'd hit the nail right on the head so quickly, but she was not about to admit anything of the kind to someone who was, after all, still a stranger.

She tossed her hair over her shoulder. "Out to build the very best damn hotel that I can," she corrected.

Her voice sounded a little too formal and removed to her own ear. After all, the man had just been nice to her. She shouldn't be treating him as if she thought he had leprosy.

So after a beat, she added, "And if that, along the way, happens to prove to my father that he'd been wrong about me all these years, well, then, that's just icing on the cake."

Icing. That was what she made him think of, Finn realized. Light, frothy icing—with a definite, tangy kick to it.

Finn leaned back in his chair, scrutinizing the woman he'd brought to the diner. The next few months were shaping up to be very interesting, he decided.

Chapter Five

"How would you like to come and work for me?"

The question caught Finn completely off guard, but he was able to keep any indication of his surprise from registering on his face.

Rather than laughing or turning the sexy-looking woman down outright, he decided to play along for a little while and see where this was going.

"Doing what?" he asked her, sounding neither interested nor disinterested, just mildly curious as to what was behind her offer.

He'd lowered his voice and just for a split second, Connie felt as if they were having a far more intimate conversation than one involving the construction of the town's first hotel.

His question caused scenarios to flash through her brain, scenarios that had absolutely *nothing* to do with the direction of the conversation or what she was attempting to accomplish.

Scenarios that included just the two of them—and no hotel in sight.

She'd never had anything that could be labeled as an actual *relationship,* but it had been a while between even casual liaisons. The truth of it was, she'd gotten so involved in trying to play a larger part in the construction company, not to mention in getting her father to come around, she'd wound up sacrificing everything else to that one narrow goal.

And that included having anything that even remotely resembled a social life.

Just now, she had felt the acute lack.

The next second, she'd banished the entire episode from her mind.

Without realizing it, she wet her lips before answering his question. "I want you to head up my construction crew for the new hotel."

She might not have been aware of the small, reflexive action, but Finn definitely was. It drew his attention to the shape of her lips—and the fleeting impulse to discover what those lips would have felt like against his own.

Reining in his thoughts, Finn focused on what she had just said. The only conclusion he could reach was that she had to be putting him on.

"The fact that I've never headed up a construction crew before doesn't bother you?" he asked, doing nothing to hide his skepticism.

Connie shrugged carelessly.

"There always has to be a first time," she told him.

That wasn't his point. "Granted, but—"

She wanted him for the job, but there had to be others in this blot of a town who were qualified for the position. What she'd seen at Murphy's convinced her of his leadership qualities. She was not about to beg.

"Look, if you don't want the job, just say so. I'll understand."

He raised his hand to stop her before she could go off on a tangent—or for that matter, leave. When he came right down to it, he'd be more than happy to accept her offer. But there were extenuating circumstances—even if he was to believe that she was really serious.

"Trust me," he told her, "it's not that I don't want to."

If this had been a legitimate offer, he would have snapped it up in an instant. He'd had a chance to compare how he felt when he was working on making something become a tangible reality—first the bathroom for the room above the saloon, and then restoring and renovating Brett's ranch house. He had to admit that was when he felt as if he'd come into his own, when he felt as if he'd finally found something he enjoyed doing that he was really good at.

Those were all reasons for him to pursue this line of business—God knew there was more than enough work for a builder in the area.

But that notwithstanding, Constance Carmichael had no way of knowing any of that. The woman had only been in Forever a few hours, not nearly enough time to orient herself about anyone or anything. Besides, there wasn't anyone to talk to about the quality of work he did because Brett—and Alisha— were the only ones who would have that sort of input for this woman. As far as he knew, Connie hadn't talked to either one of them about him—or about anything else for that matter.

Since she'd seen for herself that strangers really *were* rare in Forever, her fishing around for workers would have instantly become the topic of conversation.

He had no doubt that now that they had left Murphy's, the rest of the patrons were busy talking about the hotel that she had come to build. The skeptics would maintain that the project would never get off the ground because Forever didn't need a hotel, while the hopefuls would declare that it was high time progress finally paid Forever a visit.

Every one of those patrons would secretly be hoping that the promise of extra employment would actually find its way to Forever, at least for the duration of this project.

And he was definitely in that group.

"It's just that," he continued honestly, "I don't quite understand why you would want me in that sort of capacity."

The simple truth was that Connie had good gut instincts, and she'd come to rely on them.

"When I drove by the ranch house this morning, I liked what I saw."

The second the words were out of her mouth, Connie realized what they had to have sounded like to Finn. It was a struggle to keep the heat from rising up her cheeks and discoloring them. She did her best to retrace her steps.

"I mean, you looked like someone who knew what he was doing." That still didn't say what she wanted to say, Connie thought in frustration.

She tried again, deliberately refraining from apologizing or commenting on her seemingly inability to say what she meant. She did *not* want this cowboy bartender getting the wrong idea.

Trying it one more time, Connie cleared her throat and made one last attempt at saving face as well as stating her case.

"What I'm trying to say is that I was impressed with what you had apparently done with the ranch house you said that your brother inherited."

"How do you know what I did and what was already there?" Finn asked.

"When you've been in the construction business for as long as I have, you develop an eye for it," she told him.

Finn didn't bother challenging that outright, instinctively knowing that she would take it as a personal attack on her abilities.

But what he did challenge was her timeline, her claim to having years of experience.

"And just how long have you been *in the business?*" he asked. "Ten weeks?" he hazarded a guess, given her fresh appearance and her less than orthodox approach to the work.

Connie's eyes narrowed. Maybe she was wrong about this cowboy. "Try more like ten years."

Finn stared at her. The woman before him was far too young to have had that many years invested in almost *anything* except for just plain growing up. "You're kidding."

"Why would I joke about something like that?" she asked, not understanding why he would ever *think* something like that. "I got a job in the company right out of high school, working part-time. What that amounted to was any time I wasn't in college, working toward my degree, I was on one site or another, learning the trade firsthand."

Since she'd brought the subject up, he was curious. "What was your major in college?"

"It was a split one, actually," she answered. "Architecture and engineering. And I minored in business," she added.

New admiration rose in his eyes as he regarded her. "A triple threat, eh?"

She didn't see herself as a triple threat, just as prepared—and said so. "I wanted to be prepared for any possibility."

Finn nodded. His opinion of her was taking on a different form. The woman sitting opposite him, seemingly enjoying a rather cheap dinner, was multidimensional. To begin with, she had the face of an angel and the body, from what he could tell, of a model.

If she wasn't exaggerating about her background, the woman wasn't just a triple threat, she was a barely harnessed dynamo.

"Well, I think you've covered that," he told her with no small appreciation.

Because of her father, Connie was accustomed to being on the receiving end of a great deal of empty flattery uttered by men who wanted to use her as a way to get ahead with her father. She would have been inclined to say that was what was going on now, but something told her that Finn Murphy wasn't given to offering up empty flattery—or making empty gestures, either. That put his words under the heading of a genuine compliment.

"Thank you," she said quietly.

Finn leaned across the table. "Let's say, for the sake of argument, that I'm interested in working for you," he began. "Exactly what is it that you see me doing?"

"What I already said," she told him. "Heading up the work crew."

"You mean like telling people what to do?"

She nodded. "And seeing that they do it," she added with a hint of a smile. "That's a very important point," she underscored.

This didn't seem quite real to him. Who did business this way, just come waltzing into town, making snap decisions just by *looking* at people?

"And you really think I'm the one for the job by spending fifteen minutes looking at my handiwork on the ranch house?" he asked her incredulously.

"That and the way you handled yourself at the bar," she told him.

"You intend to have me serve drinks on the job?" he asked wryly. In actuality, he had no idea what his job at Murphy's would have to do with the job she was supposedly hiring him for.

"The way you handled *the men* at the bar," Connie corrected herself, emphasizing what she viewed was the crucial part. "You have an air of authority about you—it's evident in everything you do. And just so you know, that air of authority doesn't have to be loud," she told him, second-guessing that he would point out that he had hardly said a word and when he had, none of the words had been voiced particularly loudly.

"The upshot of all this is that men listen to you," she concluded.

She was thinking specifically of the man who had tried to hit on her at the bar. Finn had made the man back off without causing a scene of any sort, and she appreciated that— and saw the merit in that sort of behavior— on many levels.

"When's this job supposed to start?" he asked. "Brett's getting married in a couple of months. I can't just leave him high and dry. He needs someone to run Murphy's while he and Alisha are on their honeymoon."

She assumed that *Alisha* and the woman he had referred to earlier as *Lady Doc* were one and the same, although she wasn't really interested in names.

"We can make arrangements regarding that when the time comes," she promised. "Besides, I gather that most of the business at Murphy's is conducted after six." She raised a quizzical eyebrow, waiting for his confirmation.

"Most of it," Finn agreed. "But not all of it. Brett opens the doors officially at noon, just in case someone really needs to start drowning their sorrows earlier than six."

"There's a third brother, right?"

"Liam's more into providing the music for Murphy's than he is into actually serving the drinks."

"But he can, right?"

Finn inclined his head. "Right."

That meant the solution to Finn's problem was a very simple one.

"Then you or Brett tell Liam that his services as a bartender are more important than his playing whatever it is that he plays."

"Guitar," Finn prompted. And family pride had him adding, "And he's pretty damn good. A better musician than a bartender," he told her.

That might be so, but in her estimation, this third brother's talent was not the source of the problem. Apparently, Finn needed a little more convincing.

"I guess it all boils down to what do *you* want more? To continue working at the bar, or to stretch your wings and try doing something new, try challenging yourself," she urged. "Maybe," she concluded, "it's time to put yourself first for a change."

What she had just suggested he saw as being selfish and self-centered. "That's not how family works," he told her.

"That's *exactly* how family works," she corrected with feeling. "*If* the members of that family want to get ahead in the world," she qualified, her eyes meeting his, challenging him to say otherwise.

For a moment, Finn actually thought about terminating the informal meeting then and there. He debated getting up and walking out, but then he decided that the young woman with the blue-diamond eyes apparently was here on her little mission and that if someone didn't come to her aid and pitch in, this whirling dervish in a dress would spin herself right into a huge pratfall—and a very painful one at that.

But first, she needed to be straightened out.

"I think there's something you have to realize," he told her in a slow, easy drawl that belied what he felt was the seriousness of his message.

"And that is…?" she asked.

"The people in Forever aren't really all that interested in 'getting ahead in the world' as you put it," he told her. "If they were, they would have left the area when they graduated high school, if not sooner. We're well aware that there's a big world out there, with bigger opportunities than Forever could *ever* possibly offer.

"But that's not what's important to us," he stressed, looking at her to see if he was getting through to her at all. It wasn't about the money or getting ahead; it was the pride in getting something done and done well. "You might find that bit of information useful when you're working with us."

This is a whole different world, Connie couldn't help thinking. It was totally foreign from anything she was accustomed to. But there was a bit of charm to this philosophy, to this way of viewing things—she just didn't want that *charm* getting in the way of her end goal: completing the hotel and ultimately getting it on its feet.

"I appreciate you sharing that with me," she told Finn.

He grinned. He could still read between the lines. "No, you don't. You think what I'm saying is hopelessly lazy at its worst. Horribly unproductive at its very best."

"Fortunately, I don't have to think about

it at all," she told him, then smiled broadly. "Because I have you for that—" And then she realized that he still hadn't accepted the job in so many words. "Unless you've decided to turn down my offer."

"It's not an offer yet," he pointed out to her. "It's only a proposition. To be an offer," he explained when she looked at him in confusion, "you would have had to have mentioned a salary—and you haven't."

"You're right," Connie realized, then nodded her head. That, at least, could be fixed immediately. "My mistake." She rectified it in the next breath by quoting Finn a rather handsome salary.

"A month?" Finn asked, trying to put the amount in perspective. She had just quoted a sum that was a more than decent amount.

Connie shook her head. "No, that's payable each week," she corrected.

Finn stared at her. It was all he could do to keep his jaw from dropping open. The amount she'd quoted was enough to cause him to stop breathing for a moment, sincerely trying to figure out if he was dreaming or not.

"A week," he repeated, stunned at the amount of money that was being bandied about. "For someone with no work experience in the field?" he asked incredulously.

She had to be testing him, he concluded. To what end he had no idea, but nobody really earned that sort of money in a week, not unless they were crooked.

"You have life experience," she countered. "That trumps just work experience seven ways from Sunday."

Hearing the phrase made him grin.

"What?" she asked.

"Nothing." He began to wave the matter away, then stopped. What was the harm of sharing this? "It's just that I haven't heard that phrase since my mom died. She liked to say it," he confessed.

That in turn brought a smile to *her* lips.

Small world, Connie couldn't help thinking. The phrase had been a common one for her own mother.

"Wise lady," she said now.

"I like to think so." Finn gave it less than a minute before he nodded his head. "She would have liked you," he told Connie. And as far as he was concerned, that cinched it for him. Besides, it wasn't like he was signing away the next twenty years of his life.

Putting out his hand, Finn said to her,

"Well, Ms. Carmichael, looks like you've got yourself a crew foreman."

Connie was fairly beaming when she said to him with relish, "Welcome to Carmichael Construction," and then shook his hand.

Chapter Six

"Well, you two seemed to have come to some sort of an amicable agreement," Miss Joan noted.

Having covertly observed the two occupants of the table from a discreet distance for the duration of their conversation, Miss Joan decided that now was the proper time to approach them.

Not that she was all that interested in restraint, but this was someone new to her, and she wanted to start out slowly with the young woman. Picking up a coffeepot as she rounded the counter, she used that as her excuse to make her way over to their table.

It was time to see if either of their coffee cups was in need of refilling. High time.

Pouring a little more coffee into both their cups, Miss Joan looked from the young woman to Finn. They had dropped their hands when she had come to their table and had now fallen into silence.

Silence had never been a deterrent for Miss Joan. On the contrary, it merely allowed her to speak without having to raise her voice.

"Anything I might be interested in knowing about?" the older woman asked them cheerfully.

Connie could only stare at the other woman, momentarily struck speechless. Granted, she was accustomed to her father's extremely blunt approach when he wanted to know something. The man never beat around the bush. His demand for information was nothing if not direct.

However, everyone else she'd ever dealt with was far more subtle about their desire to extract any useful information from her.

Miss Joan, apparently, was in a class by herself. Polite, but definitely not subtle.

Since she was in Forever for the singular purpose of getting this hotel not just off the ground but also completed, and to that end she was looking to hire local people, Connie told herself that she shouldn't feel as if her privacy had been invaded—even though she had a feeling that Miss Joan would have been just as straightforward and just as blunt with her query.

You're not here to make lasting friendships—just to get the hotel erected, Connie told herself sternly. *Act accordingly.*

So Connie smiled at Miss Joan, a woman her gut instincts told her made a far better ally than an enemy, and said to her, "Mr. Murphy here has just become my first hire."

Miss Joan's shrewd eyes darted from Finn back to the young woman. "You're looking to hire men?" she asked with a completely unreadable expression.

Finn could see that Connie's simple statement could easily get misinterpreted and even once it was cleared up, there would undoubtedly be lingering rumors and repercussions. He came to Connie's rescue before she could say anything further.

"Ms. Carmichael is going to be building a hotel in town, and she's looking to hire construction workers," Finn told Miss Joan succinctly.

Miss Joan leaned her hip against the side of the table, turning his words over in her head.

"A hotel, eh? Something tells me you'll get the show on the road a hell of a lot quicker if you two stop referring to each other as *Ms.* and *Mr.* and just use each other's given names." And then she considered the project Finn had mentioned a moment longer. Her approval wasn't long in coming. "Might not be a bad idea at that, putting up a hotel around here. Give people a place to stay if they find themselves temporarily in Forever for one reason or another."

She straightened up then and looked directly at the young woman. "Speaking of which, where is it that you're going to be staying for the duration of this mighty undertaking, honey?" she asked.

Connie wasn't used to being accountable to anyone but her father, so it took a second to talk herself into answering. The woman was just being nosy.

"I've got a room reserved at the hotel in Pine Ridge," Connie replied, thinking how ironic that had to sound to anyone who was listening.

"Pine Ridge?" Miss Joan repeated incredulously. The expression on her face went from disbelief to dismissive. "That's at least fifty miles away from here. You can't be driving fifty miles at the end of the day," Miss Joan informed her authoritatively. "You'll be too damn tired, might hit something you didn't intend to."

As opposed to something she *had* intended to hit? Connie wondered. She shrugged in response. "I'm afraid it can't be helped."

"Sure it can," Miss Joan insisted. "You can come and stay with me and my husband. I've got an extra bedroom you can have. No trouble at all," she added as if the discussion was over and the course of action already decided.

But it wasn't decided at all. Again, Connie could only stare at the other woman, completely stunned. How could this Miss Joan just come out and offer her a bed under her roof? Things like that just weren't done where she came from.

Wasn't the woman afraid she might be taking in a thief—or worse? Apparently, people around here were far less cautious.

"But you don't know me," Connie pointed out.

Miss Joan snorted as if that made no difference at all.

"Finn here seems to trust you, and that's

good enough for me," the older woman told her. "Besides, you just said you were building a hotel here. That'll put some of our boys to work, earning more money than they have in a long while, and that's *really* good enough for me. Especially if you include some of those boys on the reservation. They're a proud bunch, but they need work just like the others." Miss Joan leveled a gaze at the younger woman. "Whatever you need," she told Connie, "you come check with me first. I'll see that you get it."

With that, Miss Joan took her leave and sauntered away.

Finn could almost see what his table companion was thinking by the stunned expression on her face. Survivors of a hurricane had the exact same expression.

"Well, that's Miss Joan all right," he commented. "She's pretty much a force of nature. But she means well. She comes through, too. And just so you know, you wouldn't be the first person who's stayed with her when they first came to town."

Connie didn't care if the woman had a guest registry a mile long, she wasn't about to accept anyone's charity. "Thanks, but I do have that hotel room reserved, and I don't mind the drive."

The latter statement wasn't really true. Connie very much *did* mind the drive, especially since she was going to be doing it at night. She was, perforce, independent, but that didn't mean that she wouldn't have preferred not having to drive a long, lonely, relatively unknown stretch of road in the dark. But she had no choice—unless she got a pup tent and camped out.

What she *did* plan on getting sent down, once the work got under way, was an on-site trailer. She'd definitely be able to sleep in it. That way, all she'd have to do was step outside her door, and she would be at work. And once her day was over, her bed wouldn't be far away.

"Suit yourself," Finn was saying. "But if I know Miss Joan, her offer stands and will continue to stand until either the hotel is finished or you actually move into someone's place here in Forever."

Connie paused for a moment, captivated by what he was saying despite the fact that her mind was racing around a mile a minute, pulling together myriad details and things she had to take care of before this work got fully under way.

She was having a hard time accepting what he was telling her. "Are you people really this open and generous?"

The corner of Finn's mouth rose in an amused semismile, just like the one, he was told, that on occasion graced his older brother's face.

"I wouldn't know about open and generous," he confessed. "We see it as business as usual," Finn told her matter-of-factly. "Everyone just looks out for everyone else here in Forever."

Any moment now, the people here were going to join hands and sing, Connie thought sarcastically.

"Yes, but I'm not an insider," she pointed out—needlessly, in her opinion. "I'm an outsider."

He laughed at her statement. "An outsider is just an insider who hasn't come in yet," Finn informed her very simply.

He was kidding, right? "That's very quaint," she told him.

He took no offense at the dismissive note in her voice. Finn had learned that some people needed a little more time to come around. He had no doubts that once her hotel was framed, she would see things differently. He could wait.

"And also true," he added.

"If you say so." Connie looked down at her plate. Dinner had somehow gotten eaten without her taking much note of it or of the process of consuming it.

Okay, it was time to call it a day for now, Connie decided. She discreetly pushed back her plate, away from her.

"Thank you for dinner," she told him, rising to her feet. "I'm going to start heading back to Pine Ridge now, but I'll be back here in the morning. We can start signing up workers then."

Finn was on his feet, as well. Knowing the prices on the menu by heart, he took out several bills and left them on the table.

"Sounds good." Getting up from the table, he walked her to the front door, acutely aware that Miss Joan was watching their every move, no matter where she was in the diner. "Where do you plan to set up?"

She stepped across the threshold. "Set up?"

He nodded. "I figure I can spread the word, round up a bunch of people for you to interview, but you're going to need to set up somewhere so you can conduct these interviews."

He was right; she needed a central place, somewhere everyone was familiar with and felt comfortable in. It took Connie less than a minute to think of the perfect place.

"How about at Murphy's? Could you open early for me?" she asked, turning directly toward him. "I could conduct interviews there, although if you vouch for the people you bring to me, I don't foresee the interview process taking very long."

She supposed that her father would have accused her of being crazy. She'd had just met this man, and she was behaving as if he was a lifelong trusted friend. But there was just something about Finn Murphy that told her he was the kind of man who always came through, who wouldn't let a person down, not even for his own personal gain. If he told her that someone was worth hiring, she saw no reason to doubt his assessment.

"Murphy's is doable," he told her.

Brett might take some convincing, Finn thought, but he had no reason to think that his brother wouldn't come around. After all, this was ultimately for the good of the town, something that always interested Brett.

"How soon are you looking to get started?" he asked.

"Yesterday," Connie answered.

He believed her.

"Then *we* have some catching up to do," he told her, walking her to her car.

It was a long drive, Connie thought as she *finally* saw the lights of Pine Ridge come into view in the distance.

It wasn't a drive she relished. Maybe she'd see about having that trailer brought in as soon as possible. Granted, the road between Forever and Pine Ridge was pretty empty, but that didn't mean she couldn't find herself accidentally driving into some sort of a ditch, especially if she fell asleep. The road was exceedingly deserted and boring. Monotony put her to sleep, hence her problem.

Mornings wouldn't be a problem. She'd be fresh in the morning, far less likely to have an accident. But even so, it was still time wasted, time she was taking away from getting the actual hotel completed.

For the good of the job, Connie began to seriously entertain taking Miss Joan up on her offer. God knew she valued her privacy, and she liked keeping to herself, separating the public Connie from the private one, but this

was business and, as such, she was willing
to sacrifice a lot of her own personal beliefs.

Anything to show her father she could live
up to her word and be the asset to the company he was always saying he wanted.

The first thing she did when she got into
her room at the hotel—besides immediately
kick off her shoes and allow her toes to sink
into the rug—was place a call to her father's
business manager on her cell phone.

Stewart Emerson answered on the second
ring. "Hello?"

The familiar, deep voice vibrated against
her ear, magically creating a comfort zone
for her. "Stewart, it's Connie."

Instant warmth flooded his voice. "By the
tone of your voice, I take it that all systems
are a go."

She laughed. Good old Stewart. The man
seemed to be able to read her thoughts before she ever said anything. She'd discovered
long ago that a simple hello could tell the man
volumes.

Ever since she could remember, Emerson
was like the father that Calvin Carmichael
wasn't, the man who made her feel that she
had a safety net beneath her if she ever really needed one.

She knew without being told that he had her back in every project she had ever gotten involved in. He'd always made sure that her father only received the positive reports.

Granted, the senior Carmichael paid his salary, but Calvin Carmichael's lifelong associate reasoned that his boss's daughter had a great deal to contend with as it was; he just wanted to make it a little easier for her. He knew the sort of demands that Carmichael placed on his daughter—and he also knew that each time she came close to meeting those demands, Carmichael would raise the bar that much higher.

He had watched her grow from a little girl to the woman she had become. Watched, too, as she heartbreakingly attempted to cull and gain her father's favor, only to fail, time and again. Carmichael was the type to drive himself—and everyone in his world—hard. It made for a very successful businessman—and, at the same time, a rather unsuccessful human being.

Emerson strived to somehow prevent the same sort of fate from ultimately finding Carmichael's daughter.

"So tell me how everything's going," Emerson encouraged.

"I found someone in town who's willing to help hire the right people for the crew," she told him.

"Does he have any kind of experience with construction?" Emerson asked her.

"I came across him rebuilding a ranch house. I was really impressed with what I saw," she told him.

"Are you talking about the man, or the job he did?" He put the question to her good-naturedly.

"The job he did. I don't have time for that other stuff," she told him.

"Maybe you should make time," Emerson tactfully suggested.

"Someday, Stewart," she promised strictly to placate the man. "But not today. Anyway, from the looks of it, the man seems pretty skilled."

"And you can work with him?" Emerson questioned.

"I think so," she answered honestly. There was only one problem in the foreseeable future. "But I'm still worried that it might be hard meeting the deadline Dad set down."

"You'll do it," Emerson told her with no hesitation whatsoever.

"Thanks, Stewart." And then, radiant even

though there was no one to see her, or to appreciate the sight, she added, "Hearing you say that means a lot to me."

"I'm not just saying it, Connie. I know you. You're just as determined and stubborn to succeed as your old man. The only difference is that you're still human," he qualified. And then he warned her, "Don't drive yourself too hard."

She smiled to herself. "I won't."

There was a slight pause, and then he asked her, "Are you remembering to eat?"

Connie caught herself laughing at that. "Now you're beginning to sound like my mother."

"There are worse people to sound like," Emerson responded. There was a fond note in his voice, the way there always was when the conversation turned toward her mother.

Connie had long suspected that there had been a connection between Emerson and her mother. He'd never actually said as much, and she hadn't asked him. But one day, Connie promised herself, she intended to ask him. Not to pry, but to feel closer to not just her mother, but to the man she was speaking with, as well.

Her father had been no kinder to her mother

than he had been to her brother, or to her. It would make her feel better to know that while she was alive, her mother'd had an ally in Stewart, someone she could turn to for emotional support, even if not a single word had been exchanged between them at the time.

That was Stewart Emerson's power, she thought now. He could make a person feel safe and protected without saying a single word to that effect. He conveyed it by his very presence.

"How about the supplies?" she asked, suddenly stifling a yawn. "Are they still coming?"

"They're already on their way," Emerson confirmed. "Now if you've had dinner, I suggest you get to bed and get some rest. If I know you, you're going to drive yourself relentlessly tomorrow—and all the tomorrows after that," he added.

Because no one ever fussed over her, she allowed herself a moment just to enjoy Stewart behaving like an overprotective mother hen.

"Been looking into your crystal ball again, Stewart?"

"Don't need one where you're concerned, Connie," he told her. "I know you like a book."

She didn't bother stifling her yawn this time. Instead, still holding her cell phone to her ear, Connie stretched out on her bed for just a moment. With little encouragement, she could allow her eyes to drift shut.

"You need new reading material, Stewart," she told him with affection.

"No, I don't. You are by far my very favorite book. You don't get rid of a favorite book, Connie, you treasure it and make sure nothing happens to it. Now say good night and close your phone," he instructed.

"Good night," Connie murmured obediently.

She was asleep ten seconds after she hit End on her cell phone.

Chapter Seven

Connie was not unaccustomed to sleeping in hotels. In the past few years, she'd had to stay in more than her share of hotel rooms, most of which were indistinguishable from the hotel room she now had in Pine Ridge. Despite all this, it was not a restful night for her.

Exhausted though she was, Connie found she couldn't sleep straight through the night. Instead, she kept waking up almost every hour on the hour. The cause behind her inability to sleep in something more than fitful snatches was not a mystery to her. She was both excited and worried about what the next day held.

There was a great deal riding on this for her and although, despite her father's mind games Connie *did* have faith in herself, she was not narcissistic enough to feel that everything would turn out all right in the end—*just because.* That was her father's way of operating, not hers.

As a rule, Connie tried to proceed confidently, but keeping what to do in a worst-case scenario somewhere in the back of her mind. She knew better than to believe that the occasion would never come up. She was also well aware that while she seemed to have the beginnings of a decent relationship going with the man in charge of the crew, she wasn't exactly home free in that department yet.

Added to that, she wanted the people who would be working for her to like her. It just stood to reason that employees worked a lot better for people they liked and admired than for people whom they feared and who rode roughshod over them. This would not be an ongoing job for the people she hired but rather a one-time thing. She had to get the very best out of them in the time that she had.

And, if that wasn't enough to prey on her unguarded mind, there was that added *thing* that kept buzzing around in her brain. She

had no succinct description for this feeling,
other than to call it unsettling. She could,
however, easily trace it back to its source:
one Finn Murphy. There was something about
him, something above and beyond his capa-
bility, his craftsmanship and his obvious connection to the men of the town.

Though she would have rather not put a
label on it, Connie had always been honest
and straightforward with people—and that
included herself.

With that in mind, she forced herself to
admit that there was no other way to describe
it. The man was sexy—not overtly, not in a
showy, brash manner, but more in an inherent
way. It was part of the fabric of his makeup.
Sexiness seemed to be just ingrained in him.
There seemed to be no way to separate the
trait from the man. They were, apparently,
one and the same. But no matter how she described it, how she qualified it, the bottom
line was that she was attracted to him.

This was going to be a problem, she
thought uncomfortably.

Only if you let it be, her inner voice, the
one that always kept her on an even keel, told
her firmly.

The internal argument continued back and

forth for the duration of her morning drive from Pine Ridge to Forever, blocking out whatever songs were being played on the radio station.

The argument was so intense, she wasn't even aware of the time as it went by. One moment she was half asleep, slipping behind the steering wheel of her car, aware that she wanted to arrive in town early, the next, miraculously, she found herself there, parking in front of Murphy's, wondering if Finn had remembered their conversation about conducting the interviews in his establishment.

She shouldn't have worried, Connie realized as she got out of the vehicle. There was a line of men that went out the saloon's front doors and wound its way down the street.

Some of the men were standing in clusters, talking, others were on the ground, sitting cross-legged and giving the impression that they had been sitting there for a while. A handful looked as if they had just stepped out of a movie about cattle ranchers from the last century, complete with cowboy hats, worn jeans and dusty boots, and still others appeared downright hungry for work.

The last group was the one she paid attention to most of all. Born into the lap of luxury, she nonetheless had an endless capacity for empathy and could just imagine how it had to feel, facing financial uncertainty each and every morning.

The moment the men saw her approaching, everyone got to their feet, their posture straightening as if they were elementary school students, lining up for the teacher and hoping to pass inspection.

Connie glanced at her wristwatch, half expecting to discover that she had somehow managed to lose an hour getting here.

But she hadn't.

She was early, just as she'd initially intended. The men were even earlier.

Butterflies suddenly swooped in, clustering around her stomach, pinching her. Connie did her best to ignore them.

Approaching the entrance to Murphy's, she greeted the hopeful applicants. "Hi, I'm Constance Carmichael. I'll be conducting the interviews today." She quickly scanned the line, amazed at how many people had turned up. Finn was to be commended— either him, or Miss Joan, she amended. She had no doubt that the older woman had been quick to pass the word along that there would be jobs available. Still, she thought it judi-

cious to ask, "Are you all here about the construction crew jobs?"

To a man they all answered in the affirma-
tive, the chorus of *yeses* all but deafening.

Connie nodded, letting the moment sink
in. She felt a little overwhelmed but she did
her best not to show it.

"Okay, then I guess we'd better get started.
Give me five minutes to get things together
and then we can begin."

Hurrying past the long single line, Connie
made her way into the saloon.

In contrast to the way it had looked when
she'd first seen it, the place was lit up as
brightly as any establishment that didn't re-
quire an ambiance for its clientele.

Finn was there along with his older brother,
Brett, and another, younger man with blond
hair. She took a closer look at the latter and
realized that this had to be Liam, the youn-
gest of the Murphy brothers. The family re-
semblance was hard to miss.

But Finn wasn't talking to either one of
his brothers when she walked in. Instead,
he seemed to be deep in conversation with
a tall athletic man with straight, thick, blue-
black hair, and skin that looked as if it would

be right at home beneath the hot rays of the Texas sun.

The other man's bone structure intrigued her for a moment. It was all angles and planes, and there was almost a regal appearance to it. The man's most outstanding feature, at least for the moment, was that he was wearing what she took to be a deputy sheriff's uniform.

Did they expect things to get a little rowdy? she wondered uneasily.

Only one way to find out, Connie decided, braced for anything.

Walking up to Finn and the man he was talking to, she greeted one and introduced herself to the other. "Hi, Finn, I didn't think you'd be ready so early. I would have been here sooner if I knew," she told him honestly. Her eyes darted over to the other man. "I'm Constance Carmichael. Is there something wrong, Officer?"

"Deputy," the man corrected her. "I'm Deputy Sheriff Lone Wolf, but you can call me Joe, and no, there's nothing wrong."

Finn joined in. "Joe brought some of his friends from the rez with him when he heard you were hiring."

"The rez?" she questioned uncertainly.

"That's short for reservation," Finn explained. "Everything gets shortened these days."

Joe had been around long enough to be aware that there were those who still viewed Native Americans differently from others. He'd come to unofficially make sure that there would be no trouble erupting due to any misunderstandings that might flair up.

"You *are* hiring, right?" Joe asked the young woman.

"Absolutely," Connie answered with enthusiasm.

She knew what it was like to have a strike against her for no apparent reason other than a preconceived—and false—notion. Contrary to some opinions, her name did *not* open doors. In some cases, it actually slammed them in her face. Her father was a powerful man, but he was definitely *not* liked.

"I'm looking for able-bodied men with strong backs who don't mind working in the hot sun for an honest day's wage," she told the deputy, summarizing exactly what her criteria was. Once that was met, everything else could be taught.

"How many men are you going to need?" Finn asked her.

"How many men have you got?" she countered, indicating that the number of positions she was looking to fill was far from small.

Finn grinned. This really was going to be good for the town. "Let's get started," he told her.

He gestured to a table he'd set up for her. He and his brothers had temporarily cleared away the others, putting them off to the side for the time being, until the interviews were over for the day.

"Let's," she echoed.

Sitting down, Connie beckoned to the first man in line.

She kept at it, nonstop, until she had seen and talked to every single man in line. She reasoned that if they could stand in line all this time, waiting to talk to her, the least she could do was interview them.

Except for a few who had shown up out of idle curiosity, or had decided after the interview that the work would be too physically taxing, she wound up hiring all the men she interviewed.

Since that number turned out to be higher than she'd initially intended, rather than work a given number of employees full-time, she'd decided to spread the work out, employing all of the men she'd hired on a part-time, as-needed basis. Some, she discovered during the course of the interviews, already had jobs and had approached this position as a way to pick up some extra money, while others were looking to this construction job as a way of feeding their families.

In making her preliminary decisions about the schedule, Connie gave the latter group the most hours while the people in the former group, since they already had some sort of gainful employment, she used accordingly.

In the end, the general schedule Connie ultimately wound up putting together looked a bit complicated, but she was satisfied that she had done the very best job she could and, more important to her, had done right by some of the town's residents.

She also found that her initial instincts involved in selecting Finn were right. Finn had remained with her through the entire ordeal. He'd stood off to the side to give her space, but he always remained close enough to be there if she decided she needed backup for some reason, or to resolve some issue.

While acting as her more or less silent second in command, he'd also gotten to observe her more than holding her own. Finn found himself impressed by the way she did business as well as her underlying sincerity. Any doubts he might have still been entertaining about her were laid to rest by the end of the long session. The woman wasn't here just to take advantage of the labor or the town.

Right from the first interview, she made no secret of the fact that this hotel was important to her, but so were the people she was hiring. She made a point of telling them that she wanted them to speak up if at any time they were dissatisfied with the work conditions or the treatment they received from a superior.

All in all, he thought that this newcomer in their midst conducted herself better than some far more experienced people that both he and Brett had dealt with at one time or another.

When the last man had finally filled out a form and given it to Connie, then left the saloon, Finn came up behind her, leaned over and said, "You look like you could use a drink right about now."

Turning her head, her eyes met his, and she allowed herself a weary smile. That had been grueling, she couldn't help thinking. Even so, she felt wired—and very pleased with herself.

"Quite possibly more than one." The one thing that hosting those parties for her father and hanging around with his associates had taught her, other than how to listen and absorb information, was how to hold her liquor.

"That can be arranged," Finn told her. "I happen to know the bartender in this joint. It's a pretty well-established fact that he's a pushover for a pretty woman's smile."

God, but she felt stiff, Connie suddenly realized. She'd been sitting so long in one spot, she felt as if she could have very well melded into the chair.

"Do you know where we can find one?" she murmured, rotating her head from side to side. She could almost hear it making strange, creaking noises.

"I'm looking at one," Finn told her very simply, his eyes on hers.

Connie caught herself raising her chin. It was a purely defensive move on her part. She was waiting for some sort of a disparaging remark to follow because right about now, she felt about as pretty as a dried-up autumn leaf.

"This bartender doesn't set the bar very high, does he?" she quipped dismissively.

"On the contrary, it's pretty much an absolute," he told her.

He realized that she wasn't being cute or angling for some sort of a bigger compliment. She actually meant what she'd said. She didn't think of herself as attractive. How was that even possible? he couldn't help wondering. One glance at her more than established that fact.

"You do have mirrors in your house, don't you?" he asked. How could she possibly not see just how really gorgeous she was? He would have been willing to bet that a number of the men who had lined up today would have been willing to work for her without any monetary compensation, as long as she was on the job with them every day.

"I don't need mirrors," she answered. "I've got my father. He does more than an adequate job of keeping me aware of myself."

He was about to say that, obviously, it was her father who was suffering from some sort of blindness, but Finn never got the chance. Their conversation was abruptly curtailed when one of Miss Joan's waitresses—Dora—walked into the saloon, clutching a large insulated carrier in both hands.

She went directly to the table where Connie had set up her *office*. Seeing that it was covered with stacks of papers, she turned toward the bar instead.

"Miss Joan said you need to keep your strength up," Dora announced, setting the rectangular carrier she'd brought in on the bar.

Unzipping the insulated carrier on three of its sides, Dora extracted what turned out to be a complete three-course meal, along with a container of coffee and a huge slice of coconut cream pie.

The pie was her favorite, Connie thought. Was its inclusion in the meal just a coincidence? Or was this a further example of Miss Joan's talked-about, unusual abilities? At this point, she really didn't know what to believe—or what she ultimately felt comfortable believing.

So instead, she pretended as if all this was just commonplace. "This is for me?" she asked, feigning surprise.

"Miss Joan told me not to let anyone else pick at it but you," Dora told her.

Dora looked at Finn. A rather sharp *no trespassing* look passed between them because the latter looked rather interested in the pie.

Flashing a smile at the waitress, Finn, along with his brother, brought over one of the tables that had been pushed to the side and set it up beside the other one.

Dora brought all the items from the carrier over to that table.

Connie moved her chair over to the new table and regarded the unusual spread. She wasn't accustomed to having anyone concern themselves with her welfare. "I don't know what to say."

"Don't have to say anything," Dora told her, zipping up the carrier and then slinging the straps over her shoulder as if it was nothing more than an oddly shaped shoulder bag. "Miss Joan said for you to consider it her investment in the hotel—and the future."

Connie was unclear as to the message that was being conveyed. She glanced at Finn. "What's that supposed to mean?"

Finn laughed. "You got me. Half the time we're not sure exactly *what* Miss Joan's saying, only that, somehow, in the long run, that very sharp lady always turns out to be right."

"I don't have any great insight in the way people think," Joe began, joining the circle of people, "but offhand, I'd say that Miss Joan just wants to make sure you don't waste away.

She doesn't like anyone being as skinny as she is," the deputy added with a dry laugh. He turned toward Brett. "I'll be heading back now." His attention shifted for a moment back to the young woman he had initially come to see this morning. "Thanks for hiring some of my friends."

"No reason to thank me." She thought for a moment, then added just before he walked toward the door, "If there's any thanks to be given, I should be the one to be thanking you for bringing them here today."

"Then you can thank Finn," Joe told her. The man he'd just mentioned had temporarily stepped aside to talk to Brett. "He's the one who told me about this hotel your company's building." He nodded, as if agreeing with something he was thinking before he said out loud, "Finn's a good man."

Connie had no intentions of disputing that. Her gut instincts had already told her the same the morning she had seen him standing before the ranch house, tool belt dipped provocatively at his hips, causing his jeans to dip with them. It had brought a whole new meaning of *fine craftsmanship* flashing through her mind.

Out loud, she murmured to Joe, "I'm beginning to see that."

The problem, however, was that she was also beginning to see a lot more, and that could only have a negative effect on her ultimately getting the job done the way she wanted to.

Chapter Eight

"I'll take that drink now," Connie said, slipping onto the bar stool.

Finn seemed somewhat surprised to see her sitting there. The woman had somehow managed to make it from her table to the bar without a single telltale sound to alert him that she was moving in his direction. Glancing around her, he saw Joe just as the latter went out the front door. He couldn't see the deputy's face from where he was—not that it would have done any good even if he had. As a rule, Joe's face was completely unreadable, giving nothing away that he didn't want to.

"Joe giving you a hard time?" Finn asked her, curious.

It took Connie a second to connect the face with the name. She'd spoken to several "Joes" during the marathon interviewing session today.

"Oh, you mean the deputy?" she finally concluded. "No, he was nice as pie."

Pouring her a shot of Kentucky bourbon, Finn moved the partially filled glass in front of her. "Not that I didn't offer you one just a few minutes ago, but why do you suddenly look as if you actually need this drink?" he asked.

She raised the glass, but rather than throw back the drink or sip it, she just studied the amber liquid in it, moving it slowly from side to side.

"So I can talk myself out of the idea that I'm in over my head," she replied.

He hadn't expected her to say that. From what he had seen, Connie Carmichael struck him as being equal to anything she tackled. But he'd learned long ago that self-image had a lot to do in making decisions that affected more than just yourself.

"Is that how you feel?" he asked.

She laughed shortly, shaking her head. "You're not much of a bartender, are you?"

Although, she silently had to admit, Finn Murphy with his lean, sculpted torso, sexy smile and magnetic green eyes was every woman's fantasy come to life. She would have to watch her step with him. Really watch her step.

"Come again?" Finn asked.

"Well, isn't this the part where you tell me that, 'no, you're not in over your head. Everything's going to work out just fine and we'll stand to gain from this experience when it's all behind us.'" Her tone of voice was only partially sarcastic.

"Don't see why I should. You seem to have taken care of that part pretty much on your own."

Connie frowned, still regarding the drink in her hand. "Yeah, except that I don't believe myself." And with that, she took a long, savoring sip from her glass. Closing her eyes, she allowed herself to focus on the fiery path the alcohol took through her body. He noted that she didn't toss her drink down, the way people would when they were trying to erase a reaction or memory of a sore point.

"Maybe you should," he told her. "From

where I'm standing, you seem like a very capable person. Notice I said *capable,* not *superhuman,*" he pointed out. "If you were shooting for superhuman, I'd say that you had unrealistic expectations. But since you're not, I'd say that everything was A-okay. Now why don't you take that drink—" he nodded at it "—go back to your table and have that dinner Miss Joan sent over before it gets cold?" he suggested. "If I don't miss my guess, Angel made that dinner special, just for you."

"Angel?" Connie tried to recall if she'd met anyone answering to that name in the last two days. She came up empty.

"Gabe Rodriguez's wife," Finn told her. "Miss Joan's got her working at the diner, and that lady's got a way with food that's nothing short of heavenly." He paused to inhale deeply even though it was literally impossible to catch a whiff of the aroma of the meal. The distance was fairly substantial. "I'd recognize Angel's fried chicken *anywhere.*"

He sounded as if he'd enjoy the meal a lot more than she would, Connie thought. Her stomach was badly knotted. As far as she knew, he hadn't had a chance to eat anything, either, so she beckoned him over before she even sat down at the table again.

"Why don't you join me, then? There's more than enough here for both of us," she told him, indicating the food that was on the table.

Finn glanced at the heaping basket of fried chicken that had been placed beside her plate. He knew Miss Joan and the way the woman thought. She had people and their appetites down to a science, and she wouldn't have sent over that much food if she thought that Connie would be eating it by herself. What he was looking at was a deliberate double portion, generous, yes, but definitely a double portion.

Why Miss Joan had sent a double portion, he could only speculate, but he had a feeling that if Connie suspected this was what the older woman had in mind—that they share a meal together for the second time—it just might be the added pressure that would cause Connie's undoing. The woman currently had more than enough on her mind without trying to fathom what was going on in Miss Joan's head.

"Well, if you insist," Finn allowed, crossing over to her table.

"I do."

"Then how can I say no? You're the boss

lady," he told her agreeably as he took a seat opposite her at the table.

Boss lady.

That sounded good, Connie couldn't help thinking. She just hoped that this wouldn't turn out to be an isolated incident.

She gazed at the food again and shook her head in amused disbelief. "Miss Joan must think that I have an absolutely *huge* appetite."

"Miss Joan likes to think that when it comes to the food she serves at the diner, *everyone* has a big appetite," Finn told her. "I think that woman feels it's her mission in life to fatten everyone up."

As he spoke, he reached into the basket for another piece of chicken—at the exact same time that Connie went to take one herself. They wound up both reaching for the *same* piece of fried chicken, which was why, just for a second, their fingers brushed against one another. Contact generated a spark that had no business being there, and no tangible explanation for being there, either.

They both pulled their hands back almost simultaneously.

"Sorry," Connie murmured. She was *really* going to have to be careful, she warned herself. Everything, including her entire future, was riding on her success with this project.

"No, my mistake. Go ahead," he urged, gesturing toward the basket. "After all, you're the one Miss Joan sent this to. It's her way of looking out for you," he added.

"Why would she even concern herself with me?" Connie asked. "I mean, not that it's not a nice feeling to know that someone cares whether I eat or not, but she really doesn't know me from Adam."

"Oh, I think she's got that part pretty much figured out," he told her with a grin. "There's definitely no mistaking you for any guy named Adam. As for the rest of it, Miss Joan likes to think of herself as a great judge of character. To give the woman her due, I don't think there was a single time that anyone can recall Miss Joan being wrong about anything."

"Bet that must make her hard to live with," Connie commented.

She knew firsthand what her father would be like under those circumstances. The man already felt he couldn't be opposed, and he had been wrong at least several instances that she knew of. Most likely more that she *didn't* know about, she was willing to bet.

"You'd think so, wouldn't you?" Finn agreed, then went on to say, "But I don't think there's a nicer person in Forever than Miss Joan. Oh, she comes off all prickly and distant at times, you know, crusty on the outside. But she's kind of like French bread in that way. Soft on the inside," he told her with a wink. "Miss Joan's got that famous heart of gold that so many people have benefited from. She thinks you're going to be good for the town, so that's why she's behind you the way she is," Finn told her.

Because her father had made her leery of being on the receiving end of praise, she'd never been one to take a compliment lightly or at face value.

"I don't know about *me* being good for the town," Connie said, "but the hotel's bound to be. If there's a hotel in town, people'll be more inclined to stop here rather than somewhere else. That means they'll eat their meals here, maybe spend a little money here—" And that was when an idea hit her. She looked at Finn hopefully when she asked, "Anything like an annual rodeo take place here?"

Now *that* had come out of left field, he thought. "Nope."

The woman amused him, she really did, Finn thought. It was obvious from the way she conducted herself that she was a city girl—even if she hadn't told him that her father's company was domiciled in Houston, she had the word *city* written all over her. Yet here she was, acting like some kind of an activities director, coming up with ideas about what she thought would be best for a town she'd only set foot in yesterday.

It took a great deal of self-confidence to come across like that—yet when he looked into Connie's eyes, he could see the slight element of fear lurking there. Fear of failure, he assumed. That kind of a thing might ultimately cause her to second-guess herself, which, in his experience, never amounted to anything positive in the long run.

"Maybe you should consider holding a rodeo here," she encouraged. God knew she could picture Finn on a bucking bronco, every muscle tense as he focused on the longest eight seconds of his life.

A warm shiver went up and down her spine. It was an effort to get herself under control and act as if images of Finn hadn't just taken over her brain.

"I'll do that," he told her with a wink, unable to put a lid on his amusement any longer. "I'll consider holding an annual rodeo."

"I'm serious," she told him, leaning in closer over the table. "That would really bring in more people to Forever."

"People who would have to stay at the hotel," he said with a straight face.

"Yes." And then she took a closer look at him. It wasn't that he thought she was kidding; he thought she had a screw loose, she realized. "You're laughing at me."

He did his best to turn down the wattage of his grin—but she was so damn cute when she tried to be so serious. "Not at you, with you."

Connie frowned. "You might not have noticed this, but I'm not laughing."

"But you will be. Sooner or later, you will be," he assured her. "One thing you should know about the people in Forever is that they kind of move at a slower pace than what you're probably used to."

Connie immediately interpreted the words to mean something that affected her. Instantly on the alert, she asked, "What are you telling me, that we're not going to make the deadline?"

"Oh, no, you'll make the deadline," he told her quickly, wanting to make sure she didn't misunderstand him. "That's a real hardworking bunch of men you just hired today."

Her eyebrows seemed to knit themselves over her narrowed eyes. Finn had lost her. "Then I don't understand…"

"People in Forever are slow when it comes to making changes. They take their time embracing progress, if you will."

"Everything has to embrace progress," Connie doggedly insisted. "If something isn't growing, then it's dying." It was one of the first lessons she'd ever learned—and it had come from Emerson, not her father.

"Or maybe it's just being," he suggested.

"Being?" she asked, not understanding what he was trying to tell her.

"Existing," Finn said, putting it another way. "In general, people work hard to make a living, and they feel that they're entitled to just sit back and enjoy that accomplishment. You know, sit back, take a look around and just be happy that they've managed to come this far and survived. It's not always about reaching the next major goal, or getting the next big-screen TV. In other words, it's not always about getting something bigger, or better, or faster. Sometimes, it's just about enjoying the prize that you have, the thing—however small—you succeeded in doing."

He realized that Connie hadn't said anything in a couple of minutes, hadn't attempted to interrupt him. Not just that, but she was looking at him in a very odd way, like he was speaking another language.

He'd overstepped his bounds, Finn thought, upbraiding himself. The woman wasn't ready to hear this countrified philosophy when all she was interested in was getting a good day's work out of them.

He tried to backtrack as gracefully as he could. "Hey, but that's just me," he concluded, easing himself out of the conversation.

But Connie continued to watch him in what he could only describe as a thoughtful, strange way. It was obvious that if they were to move on, he had no recourse but to ask her, "What?"

As Finn had talked, she'd stopped embracing the credo that had governed most of her life, and instead listened to what the cowboy was telling her. It didn't take a scholar to realize—rather quickly—that she was hearing the antithesis of her father's number one philosophy.

Her father would probably have this man for lunch—or try to—saying that if everyone was like him, the country would have withered and died a long time ago.

But maybe it wouldn't have, Connie now thought. Maybe the country would continue thriving because people were satisfied and that in turn made them happy. Was that so bad, just being happy?

She couldn't recall the last time her father, with his countless mind-boggling triumphs and successes, had been happy for more than a fleeting moment or two.

For Calvin Carmichael, it was always about the next project, the next conquest. Bigger, better, more streamline, all that was her father's primary focus. That was what had always kept him going even more so since her mother had died.

And, until just now, that was what kept her going, as well. But maybe not, Connie amended. "You sound like the exact opposite of my father," she told him.

"I meant no disrespect," he told her. "I just think that maybe there's room for both those points of view. Think about it," he urged. "Why should someone work so hard for something and not stop to at least enjoy it for a bit?" he asked.

Connie realized that he probably thought she was trying to find a nice way of saying that he was wrong. But the truth of it was, upon reflection, she didn't believe that he was. What Finn had done was succeed in making her think a little—not to mention that he'd managed to generate a feeling of—for lack of a better word—relief within her.

There *was* room for more than just her father's work ethic out there. That was a fact that was good to keep on the back burner, she decided.

"I didn't say I thought you were wrong. I just said you and my father would be on opposite sides of the fence when it came to your idea of what life was all about." She smiled, more to herself than at the man with whom she was sharing this impromptu dinner. "You might have guessed that my father is not the kind of man you could get to stop and smell the roses. He's more inclined to stomp on the roses as he made his way to the next rose-bush—just to reach it, not to try to savor it or appreciate it," she confessed.

At this point, Connie decided that a change of subject might do them both some good. This was just the beginning of their working relationship. It wasn't the time to get into philosophical discussions regarding—ultimately—the meaning of life. Or any other serious, possibly life-altering topic. Not if it didn't directly relate to the job at hand.

So instead, Connie turned her attention to the meal they were sharing. "You were right."

"About?" Finn asked.

"This has to be the best fried chicken I've ever had. Does Angel do something different when she makes this?"

"I'd say that would be a safe guess," Finn answered her. "But if you wanted to know exactly what she does, that's a discussion you're going to have to have with Angel."

She understood that chefs had their secret recipes, and she wasn't trying to pry. Her eye was on a much larger prize at the moment.

"You know, Miss Joan might do well if she thought about looking into maybe having a chain of restaurants, or selling a franchise— including this recipe and a few others in the package—" She looked at Finn, her momentum growing. "I'm assuming fried chicken isn't the only thing Angel does well."

She said this as she finished yet another piece of the chicken. Rather than become full, Connie only seemed better able to savor each bite the more chicken she consumed.

"Everything Angel makes is pretty tasty," Finn answered. "She has a whole bunch of regular customers who faithfully turn up at the diner since she came to work there."

"I knew it," she said with feeling. Plans and possibilities began to multiply in her head. "Angel and Miss Joan are missing a golden opportunity," Connie told him.

"I'll let them know you said so," he told her. "But for right now, I think you're missing a golden opportunity yourself."

"What do you mean?" she asked.

Finn smiled at her. It wasn't a patronizing smile. Instead, it was indulgently patient. The kind of smile a parent had while waiting for their child to catch on to something all by themselves after all the clues had been carefully and discreetly laid out.

But, Finn quickly realized, they came from different worlds, he and this woman, and thus had been raised completely differently, with a different set of rules to guide them. She would need more than just a hint to catch on.

"You're forgetting just to enjoy the moment. Just for a little while, why don't you forget about the project, your father and everything else and just enjoy the meal and what's around you without trying to see if you can maximize it or improve it or market it? Maybe I'm talking out of turn, but you're going to wind up wearing yourself out before you get a chance to make that mark on the world you're so keen on making."

She pressed her lips together. She hated to admit it, but Finn was right.

At least about the last part.

Chapter Nine

The next moment, Connie pulled herself back mentally and rallied. Maybe if she'd lived here, in this tiny speck of a town all of her life, her view of life might match the handsome cowboy's, but she wasn't from Forever. She was from Houston, and things were a lot different there, not to mention that it moved a great deal faster in the city. Oh, she was certain there were people in Houston with the exact same approach to life as Finn had just emphasized, but they were the people who were content never to get anywhere. To be satisfied with their small lot in life and just leave it at that.

But she wasn't. Her father had drummed it into her head over and over again: you were only as good as your next accomplishment.

Finn might not have a father he needed to prove himself to—once and for all—but she did, and until she accomplished that mission, those roses that needed smelling would just have to wait.

Finished with her dinner, Connie pushed herself away from the table and rose to her feet. "As tempting as just kicking back and savoring the moment sounds, I've got a full day tomorrow. We both do," she reminded him pointedly. "And I've still got a fifty-mile trip ahead of me."

It was that fifty-mile trip that was going to wear her out faster than the rest of it, he couldn't help thinking.

"Why don't you reconsider and just stay in town?" Finn suggested. "That way, you could give yourself a little while to take a well-deserved deep breath, relax and enjoy the rest of today before you go full steam ahead tomorrow."

He made it sound so very simple—but she'd learned the hard way that *nothing* was ever simple.

"And just where do you suggest I spend the

night?" Connie asked him. "My car's a little cramped for sleepovers," she added in case Finn was going to suggest that she sack out in her sports car.

"I wouldn't have even thought about you sleeping in your car," he told her. "That's a surefire way to guarantee waking up with a stiff neck. Not exactly the way you'd want to start out," he predicted. "Besides, plenty of people in town would be willing to put you up for the night," he assured her.

And just how did he propose that she go about making that a reality? Connie wondered with a touch of cynicism. "I'm not about to go begging door to door—" she began.

Finn cut in. "No begging. A lot of people here have an extra bedroom." Hell, until Brett and Alisha got married and moved into the ranch house he'd inherited, for all intents and purposes, he and his brothers didn't just have an extra room, they had an extra *house.* "All you'd have to do was say that you needed a place to stay and—"

He didn't get a chance to say that people would line up with offers to accommodate her because Connie cut him off. "Which is just another way of begging," she pointed out, stopping him in his tracks.

But Finn, she quickly learned, was not the type to give up easily. "Miss Joan offered you a room at her place," he reminded her. "That was without you saying anything about even *needing* a place."

She was not about to impose on anyone, or approach them, hat in hand, like a suppli- cant. "I already told Miss Joan I had a room in the Pine Ridge Hotel. To arbitrarily just ask her if I could stay at her place after that wouldn't seem right." She wanted the work- ers to trust her, not think of her as some sort of a giant sponge.

"What it would seem," Finn argued ami- cably, "is practical, and there's nothing Miss Joan admires more than someone being prac- tical."

Judging by the look on Connie's face, he hadn't won that argument, Finn thought. He gave getting her to agree to remain in town overnight another try by offering her another option to consider.

"Or if you really can't bring yourself to do that, my brothers and I have a house right here in town not far from this saloon," he told her. "It's plenty big."

She looked at him incredulously. Was he

actually saying what she thought he was saying? "And what, I should stay with you?"

"And my brothers," Finn tacked on for good measure.

"Even better," she murmured to herself, rolling her eyes. If she gave him the benefit of the doubt, best-case scenario, the man thought he was being helpful. She told herself to keep that in mind. "I realize that appearances don't count for very much in this day and age," she began, "but it wouldn't look right, my staying with my crew foreman in his house. Look, I'm not an unreasonable boss to work for, but there are certain lines that just shouldn't be crossed. You've got to know that," she said, searching his face to see if she'd made an impression on the cowboy.

Finn ran the edge of his thumb ever so lightly along the area just beneath each of her eyes. Initially, she began to pull back—then didn't.

There it was again, she realized, that lightning, coursing through her veins. Immobilizing her.

"Only lines I'm worried about seeing are the ones that are going to be forming right here, under your eyes, because you didn't get enough sleep," Finn told her in a low voice that made her scrambled pulse go up several more notches. "And that'll be in large part because of your fifty-mile, round-way trip from Pine Ridge to Forever. Seems like a lot to sacrifice just for appearances' sake."

Finn dropped his hand to his side. "C'mon, Ms. Carmichael, we're both adults," he coaxed gently. "Adults handle situations. Nothing's going to happen if we don't want it to."

If. He'd said if. *Not* because *but if. Was that a prophecy?*

Only if she let it become one, Connie silently insisted.

She supposed, in the interest of being here very early—Emerson had promised that the machinery she required to begin the excavation would be here first thing in the morning—finding a place in town to crash for the night was the far more practical way to go. And while staying with Miss Joan seemed to be an acceptable concept, the older woman seemed the type to subject to her a battery of questions. And Connie would feel obligated to answer in repayment for the woman's hospitality.

That was an ordeal she would definitely rather not face.

She slanted a glance toward the man standing beside her.

"What would your brothers say about your impulsive burst of hospitality?" she asked, covering up the fact that she found herself suddenly nervous with rhetoric.

Finn shrugged, as if she'd just asked a question that was hardly worth consideration. "Brett wouldn't say anything because when he knocks off for the night, which is pretty damn late, he usually goes home to the ranch house you saw me working on. Lady Doc stays there, as well, whenever she gets a chance. So Brett's not even in this picture if you're worried about what he thinks," Finn guaranteed. "As for Liam, well, Liam doesn't exactly think," he said with a dismissive laugh.

"What do you mean?" she asked, doing her best to be tactful in her inquiry.

The last thing she wanted to do was insult someone in Finn's family.

"Liam's just plain challenged—challenged by anything that's not a musical note in a song he had a hand in writing. In other words, what I'm trying to say is that if you're not shaped like a guitar, there's little chance that he'd even notice you, even if you stripped down buck naked and pretended you were the dining room tablecloth. On second thought," he amended, taking another look at the woman beside him, "maybe he's not really that far gone yet."

"As intriguing as that sounds," Connie began, but got no further.

Seeing his advantage, Finn pushed to the goal line. "Take me up on the offer. You'll be driving yourself plenty once this thing is in full swing. I can tell just by looking at you," he said, surprising her. "This might very well be your last chance to take in a deep breath and relax. If you don't want to listen to me telling you this as a friend, then maybe you'll listen to the man you're paying to head up your crew and tell you the way he sees things."

Connie stared at him for a moment, confused. "But that's you."

The smile he flashed at her cut right through the cloud of confusion that threatened to swallow her up. "Exactly," Finn agreed. "And the way I see it, your getting a good night's sleep is more important than you worrying about what a couple of people may—or may not— say about you staying at my house," he underscored.

Having laid out his argument, he took a step back. He had a feeling that crowding this woman was *not* the way to go.

"Final decision," he told her, "like with the project, is ultimately yours. But I'd like to think you'd respect my opinion and give it its due consideration. Otherwise, there's really no point in you hiring me. Think of it this way," he added, suddenly coming up with another argument in his favor. "You wouldn't have any objections to staying in the same hotel as I was in, right?"

"Right," she agreed warily, waiting to see where this was going.

"Well, then think of my house as a hotel," he told her, adding with a grin, "a very small, rather limited hotel."

The man really knew how to use his words. To look at him, she wouldn't have thought that he could actually be so persuasive.

"Bed-and-breakfast inns are larger than your house," she told him.

"So, after your hotel is completed, I'll see about adding on some extra rooms to the house," he told her. "You can think of it as a bed-and-breakfast inn in the making," he added with a wink.

She felt something flutter inside her chest

and told herself it was just that she was tired. Her reaction had nothing to do with the wink.

"My clothes are all at the hotel," she suddenly remembered, which, in her book, should have brought an end to this debate.

She should have known better.

Finn took a step back and regarded her thoughtfully for a moment. "Lady Doc's about your size, as is Dr. Dan's wife. One of them can lend you something to sleep in. The other can give you a change of clothes for tomorrow. And once we get the assignments straightened out for the day, I can send someone over to Pine Ridge to get the rest of your clothes." He grinned at her. "See? Problem solved."

And just possibly, a brand-new one started, she couldn't help thinking.

"So you've taken care of everything, just like that?" she asked out loud.

There was a note in her voice Finn didn't recognize, but he had a hunch that weather watchers would point out that it might have to do with a coming storm. He quickly got ahead of it—just in case.

"What I've done—just like that—was make suggestions," he told her. "You're the one who makes the final decisions and ultimately takes care of everything," he concluded, looking like the soul of innocence.

It was Connie's turn to look at him for a long moment. And then she nodded, suppressing what sounded like a laugh. She gave him his due. "Nice save."

Finn did not take the bait. "Just telling it the way it is," he countered.

Connie merely nodded, more to herself than to him. She definitely didn't want to spend the rest of the evening arguing—especially unproductively. Instead, she silently congratulated herself on going with her gut instincts. She'd made the right choice putting Finn in charge of all the others. If the man could pull off this side-step shuffle effectively with her, he could do it with anyone. After all, she had seen something in him from the very first moment she laid eyes on him, and it wasn't that he had looks to die for. It was a vibe she got, a silent telegraphing of potential that felt so strong, it had taken her a few minutes to process.

But just for a moment, she had to deal with his suggestion not as his boss, but as a woman. Looking at him intently, silently assuring herself that if he was selling her a bill of goods, she'd be able to tell, she had one more question for him.

"And you're *sure* neither one of your brothers—wherever they might roam—won't mind my crashing at their place—and don't tell me again that they won't be there. It's their place. That counts for something."

"They won't mind," he assured her with feeling.

"Okay, I'll stay in town," she agreed in pretty much the same tone that someone agreed to have a root canal done. She only hoped she wouldn't wind up regretting a decision of so-called convenience.

"In the interest of full disclosure," Finn went on, "I just want to warn you that neither one of my brothers—or I—are exactly good at housekeeping. I mean, it's livable and all that," he was quick to add, "if you don't mind dirt, grime and dust like you wouldn't believe." He looked a little embarrassed as he added, "Lost civilizations have less dust piled on top of them than some of the rooms in this house.

"The place is in sturdy condition," he went on to assure her. "Either that, or the dust is acting like the glue that's holding all this together," Finn told her with a hearty laugh.

Connie couldn't help wondering just how much of what the cowboy was telling her had more than an ounce of truth in it. Instead of repulsed, she found herself intrigued. Now she *wanted* to take a tour of this place where he had lived his entire life, just to see if it was in the less-than-savory condition he was describing.

"Remind me not to put you in charge of the new hotel's travel brochure," Connie told him with a shake of her head.

"I don't think you're going to need someone to remind you of that." And then it hit him. They were about to walk out of Murphy's, and Finn caught hold of his boss by the arm. He didn't want to lose sight of her until he had gotten at least this part straight. "Wait, are you saying that I managed to convince you?" he asked her, genuinely surprised. "You've decided that you're staying in Forever tonight?"

"That's what I'm saying," Connie answered—and then she paused. "Unless you've changed your mind about the offer."

"No way," he told her with enthusiasm. "You won't regret this," he promised.

She didn't know about that. Part of her already *was* regretting her decision. As a rule, while she remained friendly and outwardly approachable, she didn't really get too close to the people who essentially worked for her. The reason for that was that she never knew if they were being friendly because they liked her—or because they were using her to get to her father.

Not that that approach ever really worked, since her father could never even come close to being accused of being a *doting* father.

She looked at Finn, hardly believing that she'd actually agreed to allow him to put her up for the night. "So, is this the part where you go asking your friends to donate their clothes to me?"

"No, that comes a little later," he told her. "This is the part where you look up at the sky, say something about being awestruck over how there looks as if there's twice as much sky here as in places like Houston or Los Angeles, and I agree with you—even though I know it's not true. Then I tell you that if you see a falling star, you have to pause and make a wish. Sound too taxing?" he asked her, a hint of a smile on his face.

They had stopped walking again and were standing, in her opinion, much too close, at least for her comfort.

This was a mistake. A big one.

But if she suddenly announced that she had changed her mind about staying the night in his guest room, she'd seem flighty—worse than that, she'd seem as if she was afraid, and she'd lose any chance she had at commanding respect—from him and most likely, from the rest of the men working for her.

Her only recourse was to brazen it out.

Heaven knew it wouldn't be the first time.

"No, I think I can handle making a wish if I see a falling star," she told him.

"Well, then I'd say you've got everything under control."

Finn watched her for a long moment, thinking things that he knew he shouldn't be thinking. Things that would probably get him fired before he ever began to work on the project. But there was something about the woman, a vulnerability despite the barriers she was trying to rigidly retain in place, that reached out and spoke to him. It brought out the protector in him.

He wondered what she would say if she knew. Probably, *You're fired.*

"It's going to be fine," Finn told her.

Startled, she looked at him. "What?"

Connie wished she had as much confidence

in her succeeding as Finn apparently had—if she was to believe what he'd just said.

But you don't have everything under control, do you?

She felt another knot tightening in her stomach.

This had to be what opening-night jitters felt like for actors, she theorized. It felt as if everything was riding on this.

"I said it's going to be fine," Finn repeated. "For a second you looked as if you were a million miles away—and you were frowning, so I thought maybe you were worrying about the site. I have to ask—you always this nervous before a project?"

It was on the tip of her tongue to tell him that her emotions were none of his business, that she hadn't hired him to subject her to countless questions, but that would really be starting out on the wrong foot, and he did seem genuinely concerned.

"No, I have to admit that this is a first."

He nodded, giving her the benefit of the doubt. "You've hired on a good bunch of people, and they'll work hard to deliver whatever it is you need done," he assured her, then asked, "Anything I can do to help squelch your uneasiness?"

She smiled at him. "You just did it."

"Good to know," he told her.

They were outside the saloon now. Finn had gently coaxed her over to the side, out of the way of any foot traffic. He directed her attention toward the sky, pointing to a cluster of stars.

"Look." He indicated a constellation. "Isn't that just the most magnificent sight you've ever seen?" he asked.

To oblige him, she looked up when he told her to. Ordinarily, before tonight, the thought of a heaven full of stars did nothing for her. But looking up now, at Finn's request, she found herself at first interested, then deeply moved. The vastness spoke to her—and she could relate. Relate to feeling isolated, desolate and alone.

Shake it off, Con, she ordered herself. *Sentimental and sloppy isn't going to build the future. It's not you, anyway.*

"Beautiful, isn't it?" he asked again.

She couldn't very well pretend to be indifferent. Because she no longer was.

"Yes," she agreed, "it is. It kind of takes my breath away."

She heard him laugh. When she looked at

him quizzically, he merely said, "I know the feeling."

Except that when he said it, he wasn't looking at the sky. He was looking at her.

She told herself to ignore it, that she was misreading him. But even so, Connie could feel herself growing suddenly very warm despite the evening breeze.

Growing very warm and yearning for him to kiss her.

That's the alcohol talking, a voice in her head insisted. But she had only had the one drink, a short one at that, and she could hold far more than that and still remain lucid and steady.

It wasn't the drink. It was the man. But that was an admission she intended to take with her to the grave.

"I think we'd better get going," he told her. "The whole idea of you staying in town was for you to get extra rest—and if we stay out here like this any longer, I might wind up doing something that's going to cost me my job before I ever set foot on the construction site."

Her cheeks heated up and for just a second, she felt light-headed and giddy, like a schoolgirl. She hadn't experienced this sensation even when she had been a schoolgirl.

But the next moment, she regained control over herself and willed the moment to pass. "You're right. Let's get going."

Chapter Ten

"If you need anything," Finn told her almost an hour later as they stood on the second floor of his house, "I'm just down the hall." He pointed to the room that was located on the other side of the small bathroom he had already shown her.

Suddenly bone-tired, Connie nodded, murmuring, "Thanks."

They had stopped on the way to his home to borrow the things that she needed in the way of clothing for tonight and tomorrow. Finn couldn't think of a single other thing she needed to know at this point, so he began to withdraw from the room.

"Okay. Then I guess you're all set. See you in the morning," he told Connie.

Again she nodded, softly repeating the last word he'd just said, as if in agreement. "Morning." With that, Connie retreated into the room that he had just brought her to.

Closing the door, Connie took another, longer, longer, closer look around what he'd referred to as the guest room. It looked even smaller now than it had at first glance, barely the size of her closet back home. Perhaps even smaller. There was enough space for a double bed, one nightstand with a lamp and a very small dresser.

The closet itself, which curiosity prompted her to check out, was large enough to accommodate less than half the clothing she'd left at the hotel in Pine Ridge.

Yet from the way Finn had talked about the house as they drove over to it, she got the impression that this small, cramped house had seen a great deal more happiness and love than her father's seven-thousand-square-foot-plus mansion ever had.

There was a kind of worn-down-to-the-nub warmth emanating from the sixty-three-year-old, two-story house that was sorely missing from the place where she had grown up and still vaguely thought of as home.

She found herself envying Finn and his brothers a great deal.

Get it together, Con. You've got a full day ahead of you. Save the pity party for later.

Taking care to lock her door, Connie pushed the room's mismatched chair against it by way of an extra precaution. It wasn't that she didn't trust Finn, because oddly enough, she did, despite knowing the man for less than forty-eight hours. She'd been taught that taking an extra ounce of prevention was always a wise thing to do—just in case.

That hadn't come from her father, but was something that Emerson had taught her. The man at one point had worked as her father's head of security before becoming his general business manager. Emerson had always seemed to be aware of *everything*. She doubted there was a situation in the world that Stewart Emerson was not prepared to handle.

It never occurred to her to dismiss what he said as being useless or inapplicable. She looked to him for guidance the way one should a father. Emerson was the one who always had time for her.

Her father did not.

Connie remembered changing for bed—donning the nightshirt that Brett's fiancée gladly lent her. The verbal exchange between them, with Finn in the middle, had been fleeting. To her chagrin, she could barely recall what the woman had looked like.

But then, she was running perilously close to empty. Connie could vaguely remember lying down.

She didn't remember falling asleep, but she obviously had to have because the next thing she knew, she was looking at the watch she always wore and realizing that it was six in the morning.

Six?

Connie bolted upright. She'd wanted to be up and ready by five. Not because she thought anything actually needed attending to at that time, but because she wanted to be ready—just in case. It was always good to be prepared.

Happily, as far as she knew, everything was proceeding as planned. The necessary machinery was on its way and being delivered by a contractor Emerson had been dealing with for the past fifteen years, Milo Sawyer. Both Emerson and Sawyer knew that failure was not an option for her. Failure would have been worse than death. Emerson had told her that Sawyer took an oath on a stack of figurative bibles that everything would be there when she needed it—if not sooner.

Scrambling, silently lamenting the fact that she needed to sleep as much as she did, Connie was up, dressed and ready in less than twenty minutes.

Her heart kept pace by slamming against her rib cage, reminding her that she was, beneath it all, nervous as hell.

She looked down at what she was wearing. She wasn't keen on starting her first day on a brand-new site in someone else's clothes, but apparently she and Forever's first resident doctor's wife were the exact same size— just as Finn had predicted—and the woman seemed to think nothing of lending her a pair of jeans and a jersey.

Or so Finn had told her when he'd darted into the doctor's house and gotten the items for her. It seemed people just *gave* each other whatever was needed without questioning it. For the umpteenth time it struck her how very different her world was from the world she found herself operating in at the moment.

Moreover, it occurred to Connie, as she glanced in the small oval mirror perched on top of the bureau, that she was wearing something borrowed—the entire outfit—and something blue—the jersey. Not to mention, she also had on something old. Unlike her car, which she laughingly described as her lucky charm, the boots she was wearing were her one *real* concession to superstition: they were her *lucky* boots and they hadn't been considered *new* in the past fourteen years.

Longer, really, because the boots had once belonged to her mother. Unbeknownst to her father, she'd kept her mother's boots in the back of her closet and as luck would have it, when she reached her present adult height and weight, she discovered that the boots fit her perfectly. She had worn them on every occasion that something good had happened to her.

Connie sincerely hoped that they would continue exerting their *magical* influence and make the hotel's construction come off without a single hitch.

Ready and anxious to begin her day, Connie moved the chair away from the door and pushed it back against the wall where it had been. Unlocking the bedroom door, she ventured down the stairs silently.

Her intention was to slip out of the house

and drive over to the site—her car was conveniently parked in front of Finn's house. But when she came to the bottom of the stairs, the deep, rich smell of freshly brewed coffee surrounded her before she knew what had hit her—followed by the aroma of bacon and eggs, a classic one-two punch if ever there was one.

Unable to resist, Connie glanced toward the only source of light on the first floor at this hour. It was coming from the kitchen.

The debate between following her nose or leaving while there was no one watching her was a short one that abruptly ended when her stomach rumbled rather loudly, casting the deciding vote.

She went toward the light.

Finn was standing by the old-fashioned stove. He glanced over his shoulder in her direction the moment she stepped over the threshold. It was almost eerie, as if he instinctively knew she would come. He supposed that some people would have said they had some sort of a "connection." He could think of worse things than being connected to a woman who could scramble his insides just with a toss of her flowing, shoulder-length auburn hair.

"You're up," Finn declared by way of a greeting.

"So, apparently, are you," she countered, nodding toward the stovetop. He had three frying pans going at once.

"Everyone gets up early around here. If you don't, you're either sick—or dead," Finn told her matter-of-factly.

"That doesn't exactly leave a wide range of choice available," she commented.

He laughed and shrugged before gesturing toward the kitchen table.

"Sit down," he told her. "Coffee's hot. I'll pour you a cup."

"I can serve myself," she told him as she crossed to the counter.

She looked around for a coffeemaker, but didn't see one. But she did notice a coffeepot on the last burner on the stovetop.

Talk about old-fashioned, she thought. Connie dutifully poured the extra-black substance into her cup and retreated back to the table, getting out of Finn's way.

"Where is everyone?" she asked. She glanced out the kitchen window to see if perhaps one of his brothers was outside, but they weren't. The small area was desolate.

"Liam's holed up in his room, working on

another song for his band—he decided he didn't like his last couple of efforts—and I'm guessing that Brett's over at the other ranch house like I said he'd be." Finn was smiling as he turned away from the stove. "He likes the job I did renovating the ranch house so much, he decided he wanted to stay there, getting it set up for Lady Doc and him once they're married."

Holding the steaming mug of coffee with two hands, Connie made herself comfortable at the table. "Have you thought of taking up that line of work permanently?" she asked.

He frowned ever so slightly, not at her suggestion but over the fact that he had lost the thread of the conversation. "What line of work?"

"Construction, renovations," she elaborated. "That sort of thing. There has to be better money in it than there is in bartending," she insisted. Why was the man wasting his time bartending when he could be earning *real* money?

Finn shrugged indifferently. "I wouldn't know. So far, I've never been paid anything for doing that kind of work."

Connie stared at him. Had she gotten her

information mixed up? "I thought you said you installed a bathroom over the bar."

"I did," he confirmed. "But that was for the apartment above the bar—all that belongs to my brothers and me. Seems pretty silly to charge myself," Finn commented.

"And the ranch house?" she asked, referring to the first time she had seen him. He'd certainly been working hard that day. Free of charge?

"The same," he replied. "Besides, I told you, that's my wedding present to Brett and Lady Doc. I couldn't charge them," he said, shooting the mere notion down as beyond ludicrous.

She had no idea that they *made* men like this anymore. Connie looked at him with renewed admiration. "That's exceptionally generous of you."

He shrugged away her comment. "So, how do you like your eggs?" he asked.

"In the chicken," she quipped.

Finn stared at her. "Wanna run that by me again?" he requested.

She appreciated what he was trying to do, but there was really no need. "I don't eat eggs," she told him. "Never have, never will. I just plain don't like them no matter what you do to them," she added.

He nodded and said, "Fair enough. Got an opinion about bacon?" he asked, testing the waters cautiously.

There was bacon sizzling in the large skillet on the left back burner. "It smells good," she was forced to admit.

Finn's grin hinted of triumph. "Tastes even better," he assured her. Without waiting for her to respond, he proceeded to place four strips of what looked like perfectly fried bacon on her plate. But that obviously wasn't enough as far as he was concerned, so since she had vetoed eggs, he gave her other options: "Pancakes, waffles, French toast or…?"

She regarded him with what could be described as innocent confusion. "What about them?"

"Which do you want for breakfast?" he asked patiently.

He'd already gone out of his way more than was required. He might work for her, but there was nothing in the fine print about serving her hand and foot, and she didn't want him feeling as if this was part of his job description.

"The bacon is more than enough," Connie

assured the man. "I usually have just coffee in the morning, nothing else."

Finn frowned, obviously displeased with the answer. "You can't tackle a new day on just coffee," he told her. And then he seemed to study her for a long minute, as if he was making some sort of a major decision.

It took everything she had to wait him out, but she had a feeling that she could lose him if she began to ask him too many questions. So she did her best to appear patient—even if it was the last thing in the world that she was right now.

He was probably trying to browbeat her into eating. Simple enough fix, she decided. "Okay, I'll have toast," Connie finally conceded.

"Just toast?" he asked her.

She stuck to her guns. If she began giving in now, that would carry over to the work site, and she would quickly lose any ground she might have had to begin with. "Just toast," she confirmed. And quite honestly, she didn't even really want that.

Finn frowned for a moment longer then suddenly brightened—as if an idea had literally hit him—and went to work. A few minutes later, he deposited two large so-called *slices* onto her plate.

Stunned, Connie could only point out the obvious. "I agreed to toast. What is that?" she asked. Whatever it was, it was thick, and it was huge.

"Toast," Finn responded innocently, then a smile slipped through. "Texas style."

Each piece was the size of three regular slices of bread and together with what she had before her comprised more than a full breakfast in her opinion.

She sighed and shook her head, knowing that if she protested, she would wind up with something even bigger. And she had to admit that the aroma was definitely working its magic on her, arousing her taste buds. For the first time in years, she was hungry enough to eat something for breakfast.

"You know, it works better if you pick up a fork and put the food into your mouth instead of staring at it," he advised, sitting down opposite her.

He'd put a plate down for himself. Finn's plate was all but overflowing with bacon, eggs, toast and a sprinkling of hash browns.

Connie could only stare at the heaping plate

in complete wonder. "You're really going to eat all that?" she asked him.

"I *need* to," he emphasized. "If I don't, I'll run out of steam in a couple of hours—like clockwork," he assured her.

However, listening to him, Connie sincerely doubted what he'd just said. She'd come to quickly realize that Finn might appear laid-back, but the man was all go all the time.

"Who taught you how to cook?" she asked as she resigned herself to the meal before her.

She half expected Finn to say that he had picked things up while watching his mother fix meals in the kitchen.

He summed it up in one word: "Brett."

Connie blinked and stared at him. "Your brother?" she asked incredulously.

To her best recollection, her own brother couldn't boil water. She fervently hoped he'd learned how by now, wherever he was.

Finn nodded, seeing nothing out of the ordinary with what he was telling her. "Everything I know how to do, Brett taught me."

"Even construction?" she asked, thinking that perhaps she should have approached the older Murphy brother with a job offer, as well—because what she had seen with the ranch house had impressed her no end, and if Brett had had a hand in that, as well…

"Even construction," Finn echoed. "He taught me the basics. I kind of took off with it on my own after that," Finn admitted without a drop of conceit. "Brett's abilities—and vision—kind of went in a different direction from mine," Finn went on to tell her. "Let me put it this way. Brett can fix a leaky faucet—I can install a new one along with a new sink," he explained in an effort to illustrate his point. "Besides, Brett was always busy. He didn't have time to get caught up in anything fancy. He was keeping our family together, especially after Uncle Patrick died. Brett's the really practical one in the family," he added, as if that explained everything.

She tried to glean what he was actually telling her. "And that makes you what, the dreamer?"

"No, that's Liam. He's the dreamer in the family. Me, I'm just the guy in the middle." He grinned as he illustrated his point for her. "The guy not *too*."

If anything, that made things only more obscure in her opinion. "I'm sorry," she told him. "I don't understand. Not too…?" she repeated, at a loss as to what that meant or was supposed to illustrate for her.

Finn nodded then went on to give her examples. "Not too practical, not too dreamy. You know, not too hot, not too cold, that kind of thing. Always staying on an even keel, never too much of anything, just enough to satisfy requirements."

She held up her hand to get him to stop. Was that how he saw himself? That was awful. "You make it sound so bland," she told him.

Finn laughed softly. "Probably because it is."

Connie looked at the man sitting across from her for a very long, quiet moment, thinking of the way this man she still hardly knew seemed to stir her in ways that she'd never experienced before.

"Not by a long shot," she finally told him, though a little voice in her head warned her that she was giving too much away far too quickly.

"You want seconds?" he asked out of the blue. When she eyed him questioningly, trying to comprehend what he'd just asked, he nodded at her plate—which was somehow miraculously empty. When had she eaten everything? "Do you want seconds?" he repeated.

"No. No, thank you. It was all very good, but in the interest of not waddling onto the construction site, I think I'll just stop here," she told him, pushing back her plate.

That was when he took her plate from her, put it on top of his own and then carried both to the sink. Connie bit her lower lip, curtailing the impulse to offer to wash them for him.

The next moment, as she watched, he quickly rinsed off both plates and stacked them in the dishwasher.

An efficient male, she thought to herself.

She took a deep breath.

It was time.

Chapter Eleven

Looking back at the end of the day, as far as first days went, this had to be the very best one she had ever experienced. The machinery showed up early, as did the men who were to operate it. That meant that excavation and ground preparations could begin right on schedule and even a little bit ahead of it.

Because of the work schedules she had laboriously written up ahead of time, everyone she had hired knew almost from the very beginning exactly what to do and what was expected. Detailed schedules were conspicuously posted in a number of places.

The biggest surprise of the day for her occurred shortly before two o'clock.

Stewart Emerson walked onto the construction site, managing to catch her completely off guard.

Connie had been in the middle of a conversation with Finn, outlining what she hoped would be the project's progress for that week, when she heard a gravelly voice behind her call out her name.

Stopping in midsentence, she turned away from Finn to see exactly who sounded so much like the man she thought of as her rock.

Her mouth fell open the second she saw him.

"Stewart?" Connie cried in disbelief as the big bear of a man strode in her direction.

As Finn looked on, he watched the rather petite young woman being enfolded and all but swallowed up in the embrace of a man who could have easily doubled as Santa Claus—if the legendary figure had been a towering man given to wearing three-piece suits.

"In the flesh," Emerson confirmed. "I guess I'd better put you down. The men might not react well to seeing their boss whirled around the construction site like a weightless little doll." Emerson's deep laugh filled the immediate area.

With her feet firmly back on the ground, Connie made no effort to put space between herself and the older man. "I wasn't expecting you. What are you doing here?" she asked.

Finn stood by, wondering who this man was to her. He would have had to have been blind not to notice how radiant she suddenly looked. She was all but glowing and her smile resembled rays of sunshine reaching out to infinity. He'd thought she was a beautiful woman before, but what he'd been privy to before didn't hold a candle to what he was seeing now. Whoever this man was, he clearly lit up her world.

The one thing he did know was that this couldn't be the father who was always criticizing her.

"I thought you might need a little moral support," Emerson confessed, then laughed at his own words as he took a long look around the area. The entire grounds were humming with activity. "But you're obviously doing just fine—not that I ever thought you wouldn't. You don't lack for bodies, that's for sure," he ascertained.

"Did he send you to check up on me?" Connie asked out of curiosity.

There was no accusation in her voice. She knew that despite the fact that Emerson had been her mentor and all around best friend all these years, the man did work for her father, which meant that he had to abide by whatever wishes Calvin Carmichael voiced whenever possible. The last thing she wanted was to have Emerson terminated because of her. She knew she wouldn't be able to live with this.

"Oddly enough, no, he didn't," Emerson told her. "I meant what I said. I came down because I thought you might need a little moral support, this being your first real solo project and all. I mistakenly thought you might be in need of a pep talk, but here you are, all grown up and following in your dad's footsteps," he chuckled. "The old man would be proud of you if he saw this." Emerson gestured around the busy construction site.

"No, he wouldn't," Connie contradicted him knowingly. "You know that. If he were here, he'd be pointing out all the things he felt that I neglected to do, or had begun to do wrong..." Her voice trailed off as she eyed the heavyset man.

"All right, he wouldn't," Emerson con-

ceded. "But just because he's always looking to find ways in which you can improve
doesn't mean you're not doing a fine job to
begin with."

She knew what Emerson was trying to
do, and she loved him for it, but she was beginning to resign herself to what she was up
against when it came to her father—a bar that
was forever being raised no matter how great
her achievements.

"It's okay, Stewart, really," she told the
man, laying a hand on his arm. "My reward
will be in a job well-done, not in any praise
I'm hoping to get that'll just never come."

Out of the corner of her eye, she saw that
Finn was still standing just on the outskirts
of her conversation. "Oh, sorry, I guess your
visit threw me. I'd like to introduce you to
someone, Stewart. This is my foreman, Finn
Murphy," she told the older man, hooking her
arm through Finn's and drawing him into the
small circle that she and Emerson formed.

"Finn, this is Stewart Emerson, the man
who really runs Carmichael Construction
Corporation." And by that she meant the man
who provided the corporation with a heart.

Emerson pretended to wince. "Ouch, don't
let your dad hear you say that or I'll have my

walking papers before you can say, 'Here's your hat.'" Leaning past the young woman he considered to be the daughter he never had, Emerson grasped the hand that her foreman offered and shook it heartily. "Foreman, eh?" he repeated. He released Finn's hand, but his eyes continued to hold the other man's. "You've done this kind of thing before?" Emerson asked.

Connie immediately placed herself between the two men again. "Don't browbeat my people, Stewart. I wouldn't have hired Finn for the position if I didn't think he could do the job."

Emerson looked at her knowingly. "You'd hire a puppy to do the work if it looked at you with eyes that were sad enough. No offense, Murphy," he quickly told Finn.

"None taken," Finn replied, then added, "as long as you don't think that's why I have this job."

The look in the older man's gray eyes was unreadable. "So this isn't your first time as a foreman? You've been one before?" Emerson asked him.

For the second time, Connie came to the cowboy's defense.

"You're doing it again. You're browbeating.

And as to your question, Finn knows how to get men to follow orders." Which, she added silently, he did, just that he did it in his role as a bartender.

"Does he issue those orders himself, or does he let you do all the talking for him?" Emerson asked, a healthy dose of amusement curving his rather small, full mouth.

"Well, I do know enough not to get in her way if she decides she wants to say something," Finn told the other man politely.

Emerson regarded Connie's foreman thoughtfully. For a second, Finn thought that the older man might have felt that he'd overstepped the line. But the next moment, what he said gave no such indication.

"I just want to make sure that Connie's not being taken advantage of—by anyone," Emerson emphasized pointedly.

"Understood," Finn replied with sincerity. "But Ms. Carmichael isn't someone who *can* be easily taken advantage of. In case you haven't noticed, sir," he pretended to confide, "she's very strong-willed and very much her own person."

"Excuse me, I'm right here," Connie reminded the men, raising her hand as if she were a student in a classroom, wanting to be called on. Dropping her hand, she got in between the two men again, looking from one to the other. "I appreciate what's going on here, but I *can* fight my own battles, you know," she informed them, the statement intended for both of the men on either side of her. "Now, then, Stewart, let me take you into that trailer you remembered to send out for me and show you the plans I drew up. Maybe I can renew your faith in me once you review them."

"My faith in you never faded," Emerson informed her as he followed her to the long trailer that was to serve as both her on-site office and her home away from home, as well.

Finn hung back. He'd already seen the plans, both the ones that she herself had drawn up—strictly from an architectural standpoint—and the ones that the structural engineer she'd consulted with had put together.

In addition, he thought that if he tagged along, his presence might be construed as an intrusion under the circumstances.

Sexy and stirring though he found her, she was, after all, the one in charge of all this and ultimately, no matter what sort of feelings he might have for her, she was his boss. He had absolutely no business viewing her as anything else.

However, he silently promised himself, walking back to the backhoe, once this project was completed—and before she left Forever for Houston or her next assignment—he intended to carve out a little time alone for the two of them. There was no two ways about it. The lady most definitely intrigued him.

But he could bide his time and wait.

Patience, his older brother had drilled into him more than once, was the name of the game, and anything worth getting was worth the effort and the patience it took to wait it out.

Stewart Emerson had been around the world of construction, in one capacity or another, for a very long time. Ever since fate had stepped in one night, putting him in the right place at the right time to save Calvin Carmichael from being on the receiving end of what could have been a fatal beating.

He had not only pulled the drunken, would-be muggers off Carmichael, but by the time he was done, he had also sent the duo to the hospital—which seemed only fair inasmuch as their plan apparently had been to send Carmichael straight to the morgue.

Shaken for possibly the first—and last—time of his life as well as uncharacteristically grateful, Connie's father had immediately offered the much larger—and unemployed—former navy SEAL a job as his bodyguard.

As the business grew, so had Carmichael's dependence on Emerson, causing the latter's responsibilities to increase, as well.

Taking nothing for granted, Emerson made it a point to become familiar with everything that his employer concerned himself with and thus, while he couldn't draw up his own plans from scratch, he developed an eye for what was constructually sound, as well as what made good business sense.

Emerson made it a point to become indispensable to the corporation—and the man—in many ways.

But to Connie, the tall, heavyset, bearded man who could have easily been mistaken for Santa Claus these days would always be her one true confidant, her one true friend.

While for years, she had wanted nothing as much as to finally win her father's approval, nothing meant more to her than Emerson's opinion.

It still did.

"Well, what do you think?" she asked, gesturing toward the two large drawings that were tacked up side by side on the bulletin board that hung opposite the trailer's entrance. Between the two plans, they encompassed both the esthetics and the practical side of the building that was destined to be Forever's very first hotel.

Emerson spent a good five minutes studying first one set of plans, then the other. Finally, he stepped back and nodded his shaggy, gray head.

"I must say that I'm impressed. But then, I'd expect nothing less than the best from you," he told her, hooking his bear-like arm around her waist and pulling her toward him affectionately.

She laughed softly to herself, happily returning his hug. "That makes one of you."

Emerson released his hold from around her shoulders and did what he could to hide his sigh. There were times when he despaired if the man he worked for would ever realize exactly what he had and what he was in danger of losing.

"Your father's a hard man to please, Connie. We both know that. Did I ever tell you about the time that, after standing at the edge of the Grand Canyon, looking down for a good ten minutes, he turned to me and said, 'I could have done it better in probably half the time.' If your dad thinks he can criticize God's handiwork like that, the rest of us can't expect to be treated any better."

Though she gave Emerson no indication, it wasn't the first time she'd heard him tell her the story. Emerson had told it to her at least a couple of times, the first being a long time ago in an effort to make her feel better after her father had mercilessly taken apart a venture she'd been very proud of undertaking.

That was when she'd finally realized that *nothing* was ever going to be good enough to meet her father's standards, no matter how hard she tried.

But she wouldn't be who she was if she didn't keep on doing just that.

Trying.

Over and over again.

"I suppose I shouldn't care about pleasing him," she told Emerson, "but he put so much on this project turning out right, I feel that if I don't meet his expectations, that's it, I'm out of the game. Permanently," she added flatly.

"You'll never be permanently out of the

game," Emerson told her, even though he knew that was what he'd heard Carmichael tell her. "Doesn't matter what he says at the time. He needs you, needs your energy, needs you to keep going, to be his eyes and ears in places he can no longer get to. He'll come around," Emerson promised in a tone that made an individual feel that he could make book on the man's words and never risk a thing.

"Meanwhile," Emerson continued, his eyes on hers, "you seem to have put together a pretty good crew. They're moving back and forth like well-trained workers. And that foreman of yours—" He paused for a moment, looking at her significantly. "I'd keep my eye on him if I were you."

"Why?" Connie asked. "Don't you trust him, Stewart?"

Emerson heard the slight defensive tone in her voice and wondered if she was aware of it herself. He had a better-than-vague idea just what it meant in this instance. "Hasn't got anything to do with trust," he told her.

She was trying to follow Emerson's drift, but he did have a habit of going off on a tangent at times. This seemed to be one of those times.

"Then what…?"

For once, Emerson didn't hide his meaning behind incomprehensible rhetoric that left the listener baffled for days—because he wanted to be certain that she was aware of what was going on. It was one thing for him to catch her off guard, and another to have some stranger do it.

"Your foreman looks at you as if you were a tall, cool drink of water, and he had just come crawling in on his chafed hands and knees across the length of the desert."

Connie stared at him in bewildered disbelief. "What does that even mean?" she asked. Finn had been nothing if not polite. If anything, she had been the one who'd stared at him that first day.

Emerson grinned. "That means, don't work any long hours alone with the man or you might find something besides this building being created."

What would Stewart say if he knew that she'd spent the night in Finn's house? Connie couldn't help wondering. She was fairly confident that Stewart would ultimately believe anything she would tell him. However, she was also certain that he'd worry twice as much as before—for no reason.

She shouldn't worry. She trusted Finn implicitly—and more important, even though she was admittedly more than just mildly attracted to Finn, she trusted herself not to jeopardize the project.

That was what was important here. Not the blush of a possibly fleeting romance, but the project.

The hotel.

Winning this invisible wager with her father and being assured that her career with the company was a done deal. Anything else came in a distant second—if that.

"I never knew you had such a rich imagination, Stewart," she said, grateful that her cheeks hadn't suddenly rebelled and given her away. "Finn only thinks of me as his boss. There are plenty of women around for him to choose from if he has other inclinations," she added innocently.

"I think he's already made his choice," he told her pointedly.

"And I think you're being way too protective of me—not that I don't appreciate it," she added, lovingly patting the man's cheek. "So, how long do I have you for?" she asked, effectively changing the subject.

In response, Emerson looked at his watch.

"Just another couple of hours, I'm afraid. I'm flying back to Houston at four-thirty," he told her. "Your father's looking into acquiring another company to extend his domain, and I told him I'd be there to sit in on the meeting."

"Extension? Again?" she asked with a shake of her head. Wasn't it ever going to be enough for him? she wondered.

Emerson raised his wide, wide shoulders and then let them fall in a vague shrug. "Your father does have the resources."

Connie sighed and shook her head. "That's not the point. Is it really a smart move to spread himself so thin? What if he suddenly experiences a cash-flow problem? What then?"

Emerson laughed at the objections she raised because those were the exact same ones he'd raised with his employer. "And that's one of the reasons he has his suspicions that you're more mine than his." And then he went on to say what they both knew to be true. "Your father doesn't think that way, and ultimately, he's the boss."

"Still doesn't make him right."

"No," Emerson agreed. "It doesn't. But it also doesn't give us anything to fight with, either. He does what he wants to when he wants to."

Truer words were never spoken, Connie thought. She picked up a clipboard from the table. The next week's schedule was attached to that, as well.

"Well, I've got to get back to work." She paused and then quickly kissed the older man's cheek. "Thanks for coming to check up on me."

"Wouldn't have missed it for the world," he told her in all honesty. "And Connie?"

At the door, about to step out, she paused to look back. "Yes?"

"For what it's worth, I like him. Your foreman," he specified. "I like him."

She hadn't expected that warm feeling to go sweeping through her. It threw her for a second.

"Good. I'll let him know. Maybe the two of you can make an evening of it sometime," she said with a straight face.

The sound of Emerson's booming laugh followed her out of the trailer.

It was, for her, the most heartwarming sound she knew.

Chapter Twelve

Connie looked up from the wide drawing board in her trailer, startled to see Finn walking in. She knew the broad-shouldered man was only six-one but somehow, he just seemed to fill up the entire trailer with his presence. Given the size of her trailer, that was saying a lot.

"I knocked," he told her. "Twice."

She had no doubt that he had. She'd been lost in thought, oblivious to her surroundings, for the last half hour or so.

Connie merely nodded at his statement. "Is there a problem?" she asked, ready to send him on his way if there wasn't. She was having trouble concentrating, and the schedules were overlapping in areas where they really shouldn't.

He and Connie had been working closely now for the past four weeks, and he'd gotten somewhat accustomed to her being braced for something to go wrong. Thus far, nothing had. If anything, it had been the complete opposite since they'd started work on the hotel.

But that still didn't change her attitude.

"No, no problem," he assured her. "As a matter of fact, it's going pretty damn well, don't you think?"

It did look that way, she had to silently concede. Working in what amounted to two complete shifts, utilizing whatever daylight was available and relying on strobe lighting that she'd had brought in less than six days into the job, Connie had to admit that Finn and the crew had made tremendous headway. The two backhoes were kept humming sixteen hours a day until the excavation was completed.

In addition, the weather had been incredibly cooperative. They had no rain days to interfere with the schedules she'd so carefully drawn up. All that had put them ahead of schedule, something she was not about to take for granted.

"We still have a long way to go before we're done," she pointed out.

Despite everything he had said to her at the outset, he noted that the woman just did not know how to relax or even coast along for a minute. He was just going to have to keep at her, Finn decided.

"But not as long as when we first got started," Finn countered.

"No, of course not. The double shifts have gotten us ahead of schedule—but all it'll take is a few rain days and we'll backslide."

It had to be really taxing, he thought, anticipating the worst all the time. She needed to break that habit—or he had to do it for her.

"Weatherman says no rain for the next week," he told her mildly.

Connie stated what she felt was the obvious. "Weathermen have been wrong."

"Look on the positive side," he coaxed.

Easy for him to say, she thought. He didn't have everything riding on this the way she had. Connie glared at him, debating just murmuring some noncommittal thing, then decided that after the way he'd gotten the crew to operate like a well-oiled machine, maybe she owed him the truth.

So, in a rare unguarded moment, she admitted, "I'm afraid to."

"Nothing to be afraid of," he told Connie. "As a matter of fact, I was going to suggest that maybe, for once, we could keep it down to a single shift and even have everyone knock off early."

"Early?" she echoed. "Why?" Her voice instantly filled with concern as she assumed the worst. "*Is* something wrong?" she asked again.

"No, nothing's wrong," he assured her again in a soothing voice.

"Then why would they want to stop early?" she asked. The crew was being paid, and paid well, to work. She didn't understand the problem.

He crossed to her, gaining a little ground. He glanced at the papers she had spread out over the large drawing board. It was a wonder she didn't have a constant headache, he marveled. He got one just glancing at it.

The scent that he was beginning to identify with her—lilacs and vanilla—began to slowly seep into his consciousness. He assumed that it was a cologne, but maybe it was her shampoo. Whatever it was, he found it both pleasing and arousing—a little like the woman herself, he couldn't help thinking.

He'd come here with an ultimate goal in mind, and he forced himself to get back to it.

"Maybe because all work and no play...you know the old saying."

Connie laughed softly to herself. "In my house, we weren't allowed to mention that old saying," she told Finn. "My father did *not* believe in 'playing.' Or smelling the roses, or anything that didn't have goals and work attached to it."

He'd thought he and his brothers had had it rough as orphans. Despite certain financial hardships, their life seemed like a positive picnic in comparison to the one she must have had.

"Your father's not here," he tactfully reminded her, then quickly added, "and Brett and Alisha are having their engagement party at Murphy's tonight, so, if it's okay with you, everything's temporarily on hold until tomorrow morning."

She looked at him for a long moment. He wasn't challenging her, she realized. If he was, then her reaction would have been completely different. Still, she wanted to push the imaginary envelope just a little to see what would happen.

"And if I say that the work has to go on?"

He didn't look away but continued to meet her gaze head-on. "You'll generate a lot of ill will, and you don't want to do that," he said quietly.

Connie suppressed a sigh. No, she didn't. While she wanted to continue meeting and even surpassing her deadlines, the way her father's crews all did on their construction sites, she really did not want to maintain the kind of tense atmosphere that always existed on one of those work sites.

So, after another moment's debate, Connie nodded and gave her approval. "Fine, tell the men they have the rest of the evening off—but I'll expect them in on time tomorrow," she added, wanting to make sure that Finn didn't lose sight of the fact that she and not he was the one in charge.

"They will be. By the way, you're invited, you know."

She'd already turned her attention back to the schedules, which, in light of the lost shift, now had to be revised.

"To what?" she asked absently.

"To the engagement party."

That had her looking up at him again. "Oh. Well, thank you." She reached for a fresh piece of paper. Instead of using a laptop, she always liked to write her first draft of anything in pencil. "But I think I'll pass." She expected that to be the end of it.

It wasn't.

"Mind if I ask why?"

She indicated the drawing board before her. "If I'm losing an entire eight to ten hours of work, I've got to find somewhere to make it up."

To her surprise, rather than just go along with what she was saying, the way he had been since they had begun working together on the site, Finn took her hands in his and drew her away from the drawing board, saying, "No, you don't."

Stunned at the apparent mutiny, she blinked and stared at him. "Excuse me?"

"You heard me," he told her amicably. "No, you don't," he repeated, then added, "you don't have to do it tonight. Connie." He went on patiently. "It can't always be all about work."

Somewhere in the past few weeks, they had gone from his calling her Ms. Carmichael to using her first name. She wasn't sure exactly when, only that it had evolved rather naturally. She supposed that should have concerned her, but it hadn't.

However, she didn't appreciate being lectured to—especially when she knew in her heart that he was right. "Is this the *look up at the stars* speech again?"

"Think of it as the *let me take you to a party because life is more than just one big work schedule* speech," Finn told her, an amused smile playing along his lips.

She didn't want to be rude, but she couldn't go—for more than one reason. "Finn, I appreciate what you're trying to do—" she began.

"Good, that makes two of us," he replied. "Now, you're coming with me to this thing, and I'm not taking no for an answer."

Connie stared at her foreman in utter wonder. "You're actually going to give me a hard time about this?" she questioned.

"I'm going to *hog-tie* you if I have to," he corrected, "but you are definitely coming to the party."

She didn't understand what difference it made. "Why is it so important to you?"

He never hesitated. "Because you're important to me."

Her mouth dropped open. Did he just say what she thought he said? "What?"

Finn had no doubt that she had heard him the first time. Nonetheless, he went through it again.

"You heard me—and I *am* prepared to hog-tie you if I have to," he said with finality. "Now, are you going to sacrifice your dignity, or will you come along with me quietly?"

She looked into his eyes and had her answer. He wasn't kidding. She definitely didn't want to put him in a position where he had to carry out his threat.

"I guess I don't have a choice in the matter," she said.

"No," he agreed. "You don't. Besides, seeing you join the party will make the men respect you even more."

She was certain that if her work ethic didn't do it, it would take more than just joining in a toast to make her become one of the crew.

"I really doubt that," Connie told him.

She meant that, he realized. Finn shook his head, feeling genuinely sorry for her. "Then you have a few things to learn about the men who you have working for you."

But as he drew her over to the trailer's door, Connie suddenly looked down at what she was wearing. Jeans and a work shirt. She definitely wasn't dressed for any kind of a party.

"I can't go like this," she protested, digging in her heels.

He gave her a quick once-over. She looked fine to him. Better than fine, actually, though he didn't say so out loud.

"Why?"

"Because I'm not dressed for a party."

"You might not be dressed for one of those fancy parties your father throws in Houston," he told her, "but trust me, you'll fit right in here."

Connie looked at him, surprised at his assurance. "How do you know about my father's parties?" she asked.

Rather than take offense, Finn merely grinned at the woman's question. "Oh, it's amazing what you can find on the internet when you know where to look. We're not nearly as backward here as you seem to think."

Color flashed across her cheeks. She hadn't meant to insult him. It was just that Forever seemed so self-contained and removed from the world she was familiar with.

"I never thought you were backward," Connie protested.

"Sure you did. But that's okay. You can make it up to me by coming to my brother's engagement party," Finn told her. "C'mon, let's go, boss lady. We're wasting time here."

To emphasize his point, he pulled the trailer door closed firmly behind him then immediately turned around and took her arm. Smiling, Finn guided her over to his truck. As he did so, he waved to the men, who appeared as if they were all looking in his direction, and called out, "She says it's okay!"

Instantly, a cheer went up.

Finn grinned in satisfaction. "See? You're responsible for instant happiness. Feels good, doesn't it?"

She had to admit that it did.

The enticing sound of laughter coming from Murphy's reached them even before they ever pulled up before the saloon.

There were only a few vehicles, trucks like Finn's for the most part, that were actually parked near the saloon. It appeared that most of the people attending the engagement party that Finn and Liam were throwing for their older brother and his fiancée had walked to the saloon. That way, driving home would not be a problem or hazardous to anyone in the vicinity. The town jail was not built large enough to accommodate more than four offenders at a time.

Connie wasn't sure exactly what she expected to find once she walked into the saloon—maybe seeing the patrons line dancing—but what she did see wasn't all that different from other parties she'd attended. The clothes were definitely not as fancy, but there was live music, thanks to Liam and his band, and appetizing food arranged on side tables, buffet style, courtesy of Angel, Gabe Rodriguez's wife and Miss Joan's resident chef.

It was, all in all, a combined effort with everyone, first and foremost, wanting the future bride and groom to have a good time.

The warmth within the saloon was unmistakable.

Connie fully expected to feel awkward and more than a little out of place at such a gathering. She was afraid she'd be regarded in much the same light as a parent who was looking over their child's shoulder on the playground during recess.

But to her surprise, she wasn't. She was not only greeted by everyone she walked past, but she was also swiftly made to feel welcomed, as if she *belonged* here with the others, celebrating the fact that two very special people had managed to find one another against all odds.

Connie would have been content to sit on the sidelines, quietly nibbling on the fried chicken that Angel had painstakingly prepared and listening to people talk.

But she quickly realized that Finn apparently had other ideas for her. He waited until she'd had a beer to toast the happy couple—who she confided looked absolutely radiant—and had finished the piece of chicken he'd gotten for her.

Once she had put the denuded bone down on her plate, Finn took the plate from her and put it down on the closest flat surface. She looked at him in confusion. Had she done something wrong without realizing it?

"What are you doing?" she asked him.

"You can't dance with a plate in your hands," he told her simply.

Dance? He couldn't be serious. "I can't dance without one, either," she informed him.

Finn was already drawing her to her feet, away from the table where she'd left her near empty bottle of beer. "Sure you can."

Connie shook her head. "I'm serious, Finn.

I don't dance." She had two left feet, and she knew it.

But Finn obviously wasn't accepting excuses. "Don't? Or won't?"

"I won't because I don't," she insisted. With every word, he was drawing her further away from any small comfort zone she'd hoped to stake out and closer to the dance floor.

He laughed at the sentence she'd just uttered. "Practice saying that three times fast," he told her, all the while drawing her closer and closer to the area in the saloon that had been cleared for dancing.

She did *not* want to make a fool of herself in front of him.

"Finn, no, really. I'm going to wind up stepping all over your feet," she warned him.

Her excuse made no impression on him whatsoever. "They can take it. Besides, you're light, how much damage can you do? Don't worry, I'll teach you a few steps. You'll look like a natural," he promised.

Famous last words, she couldn't help thinking. Finn had no idea what he was getting into—but she did, and it was up to her to stop him before it was too late.

"Others have tried and failed miserably," she warned him.

"'Others' weren't me," he told her with a confidence that was neither cocky nor self-indulgent; it merely *was*. He took one of her hands in his and pressed his other hand against the small of her back.

"It's a slow song," he said, bringing her attention to it. "All you have to do is sway with the music and follow my lead."

All. Ha! The man had no idea what he was asking of her.

"I have no rhythm," Connie protested. She wasn't proud of it, but there it was. Connie Carmichael had less rhythm in her body than the average rock.

But Finn was obviously not accepting excuses tonight. "Everyone has rhythm, Connie," he countered easily. "You just have to not be afraid to let it come out. Now, c'mon," he coaxed, "let yourself feel the music. Close your eyes," he urged, "and just *feel* it," he stressed, gently guiding her movements.

This was an experiment that was doomed to fail from the very start, didn't he realize that? "You're going to be sorry," Connie warned him, even as she allowed herself to rest her head against his shoulder.

"I really doubt that," he assured her, his

voice low, a whisper only she could hear despite the general din in the room.

A moment later, her eyes flew open.

She could actually feel it. Not just the rhythm, the way Finn had promised her that she would, but she slowly felt the effects of the music as it seemed to seep into her.

Or was that her reaction to the way his body was pressed ever so gently—and incredibly seductively—against hers?

Connie wasn't quite sure, but she could definitely feel herself reacting to the music—as well as to the man.

Her heart got into the act, revving up its pace.

When the music stopped, Connie was almost sorry to hear the notes fade away.

Raising her head from his shoulder, she realized that Finn was still swaying, still moving his feet to a beat that was no longer there.

"Song's over," she told him, whispering the words into his ear.

"Shh," he responded, a mischievous smile playing on his lips. "There'll be another one to take its place in a second."

And then Liam, looking his way, struck up another slow song with his band. Couples around them began dancing again.

"See?" Finn said. "What did I tell you?"

"I should have never doubted you," she told him with a laugh.

"No," Finn agreed, looking far more serious than she would have thought the moment warranted, "you shouldn't have."

She wasn't sure just how long she and Finn danced like that. Three, four songs came and went, all surprisingly slow in tempo. For her, it felt like just one long, timeless melody that went on.

"I haven't stepped on your foot yet," she marveled when she finally realized that she was *really* dancing and not just keeping time with her hips.

His laughter, soft and warm, ruffled her hair ever so slightly. Ruffled her soul a great deal more.

"The evening's still young," Finn told her. "You'll have more opportunities to live up to that threat if you really want to."

She liked what was happening now. It couldn't continue and she knew it, but just for now, she was content to pretend that it would.

"Actually, I kind of like the fact that I haven't yet," she told him. "How do you do it?" she marveled quietly.

"Do what?" he asked as he whirled her around ever so gently. The movement was so subtle, he had a feeling she didn't even know she executed it.

"How do you get me to move this way?" she asked, mimicking him step for step. "I'm usually completely uncoordinated."

"Magic," he said, whispering the word into her ear. "I do it with magic."

A warm, tantalizing shiver shimmied up and down her spine, instantly spreading out to all parts of her. Claiming her.

Just the same way that the man did.

She knew that Finn was just putting her on with that answer. The funny thing was, though, just for a moment or two there, she could have sworn that it actually *felt* like magic.

Or, at the very least, she was more than willing to pretend that it *was* magic.

Chapter Thirteen

Living under her father's roof, Connie had hosted more than her share of parties and so-called casual get-togethers, all to the very best of her ability.

Initially, she'd imagined that she fell woefully below the standard that her late mother had set. Victoria Carmichael had a charming, outgoing personality and the ability to make each person she spoke with feel as if they were the only person in the room. In addition, Victoria had a way of lighting up any room she entered. While Connie knew that her father had never said as much to her mother, after Victoria's death he was always quick to point out how incredibly short of the mark she fell each time he ordered her to take over her mother's role as hostess.

Eventually, through sheer perseverance, Connie grew into the role and became more at ease with the part she had to play. However, she'd never enjoyed herself during any of those gatherings the way she was enjoying herself tonight, here in the small, jam-packed bar, talking with people her father would have been quick to judge, cut off and summarily dismiss as being beneath him.

She began the evening as an outsider and was certain she would remain that way throughout the entire night, but she hadn't counted on Finn taking her in hand, hadn't taken into account the character of the people attending this engagement party.

She'd just assumed that they would regard her as an intruder and laugh about how she didn't fit in behind her back. Instead, to a person, they all went out of their way to make her feel welcome.

She thought perhaps this was because of Finn, that this was somehow his idea, and he had found a way to convey his wishes to the others attending the party. But she never saw him signal anyone, never saw him indicate to the people around them that he wanted them to treat her with kid gloves.

In a way, the opposite of the latter happened because as the evening wore on, she was being teased and kidded, all in such a way that she took no offense and found herself responding lightheartedly.

By evening's end, she came away with the feeling that the people she worked with, the people who essentially worked *for* her, actually *liked* her. Liked the fact that she had come out of her trailer after hours to meet them on their own ground and celebrate that two of their own were getting married.

Each time someone proposed a toast, she was right there with them, lifting her own glass and adding her voice to the well-wishers. And each and every time she did, she was aware of Finn beside her, smiling at her and approving the way she conducted herself.

For the most part, she had lived without approval for a very long time.

As she finished her glass of champagne in what felt like an umpteenth toast, laughter bubbled up within her as she leaned into Finn and whispered, "You were right."

Turning to look at Connie, he nodded. "Of

course I was— About what, specifically?" Finn tagged on after a beat.

Her smile was wide and totally uninhibited. She must have looked like that as a child, Finn couldn't help thinking. "I am having fun."

"Yes, you are," he agreed with a laugh.

He noted that she was all but completely effervescent at this point. Connie leaned back a little too far, and he quickly put his arm around her waist to keep her from sliding off her stool. Finn gently took the empty glass from her hand and placed it on the first flat surface he saw on the bar, thinking that was safer than having her accidentally drop it. He knew that once this evening was behind her, she wouldn't appreciate being allowed to look foolish—or tipsy.

"Possibly just a tad too much fun," he speculated.

"There's no such thing as too much fun," Connie murmured. Standing up, she nearly went straight down, feeling as if her legs had mysteriously turned into tapioca pudding right beneath her. "Whoops." She grabbed hold of Finn by his shirt to keep from sinking to the floor. "I swear I only had one drink. Was there something special in it?" she asked, punctuating her question with a laugh that was mingled with a giggle.

"Nothing that wasn't in all the others," he assured her. And then he took a closer look at her. All her features had definitely mellowed. There was only one thing that could accomplish that to such a degree at this point. "How many have you had?" he asked her.

Finn hadn't bothered keeping track of the alcohol she consumed, but then, he hadn't thought he had to. Since she was so strait-laced, he assumed she'd keep track of herself.

Apparently, he was wrong, he realized.

"Just one," Connie said. "That's usually enough…"

She appeared so serious, it was hard for him not to laugh. "You're a cheap date." *Not that this is a date,* Finn added silently.

But he knew she'd be self-conscious later when she realized she'd been slightly tipsy, or even cutting loose. He took better hold of her arm to escort her out of the saloon.

Brett saw them leaving just as the couple reached the massive front door. Excusing himself from the people he was talking to, he quickly made his way over to them.

"Everything okay?" Brett asked, coming up behind the pair.

"Everything's wonderful," Connie answered in a gush before Finn could. "You throw a very mean party," she told the oldest Murphy brother.

"Actually, Finn here and Liam threw it," he gently corrected, "but on their behalf, thank you," Brett responded with a smile as he looked at her. Raising his eyes to Finn, he asked, "Are you taking her out for some air?"

"And then home," Finn added.

Connie whirled around to look at him. "You're taking me to your home?" she asked, visibly beaming. "Good, I've missed it."

Her comment took both men by surprise, especially since her stay at the ranch house had been limited to a single day.

"She's not going to remember saying that in the morning," Finn told his brother.

The latter nodded. Finn had cut her off just in time. "You need any help?" he asked Finn.

Finn smiled as he slanted a glance at the petite woman. "She's a live wire, but I can always tuck her under my arm if I have to."

"Good luck," Brett said before he turned back to the party.

"Why do you need luck?" Connie asked as Finn took her outside. And then she suddenly grinned from ear to ear. "Oh, I get it.

You're looking to get lucky. Why didn't you say so?" she asked with a laugh.

"Because I'm not looking to get lucky," he told her patiently, although the idea of getting lucky with her had more than a little to recommend it. He forced himself not to think about it. He'd only be torturing himself. "I'm just looking to get you home."

"Where you'll have your way with me," she concluded with a nod of her head, as if it were already a foregone conclusion.

Finn watched as she got into the passenger side of his vehicle. "I'm not looking for that, either," he told her matter-of-factly, doing his best to bury the fact that this new uninhibited version of her was beginning to stir him.

"Why not?" she asked, confusion highlighting her expression. "Why don't you want to have your way with me? Don't you think I'm pretty?"

They were driving now, and Finn stepped down harder on the gas pedal, going faster than the posted speed limit, but just this once. He figured he could be forgiven for that. There was no one else out on the streets and the entire sheriff's department was back at Murphy's, anyway. He needed to get Connie back to her trailer before his restraint dissolved just like soap bubbles in the spring air.

Because she was staring at him, waiting for an answer, Finn finally said, "Yes, I think you're pretty. Beautiful, actually," he amended.

"But you don't want me," she concluded sadly.

She was making it very, very difficult for him. "You're my boss," he told her, hoping that would be the end of it.

"I know that, but you can still want me," she insisted.

He could almost *feel* his defenses crumbling. "Okay, I want you. But that still doesn't mean I'm going to do anything. It wouldn't be right," he informed her firmly.

He put his truck into Park. They'd arrived at her trailer none too soon, he thought, because he was quickly losing this battle of good intentions allied with restraint. She kept leaning into him, despite the seat belt that should have kept her on her side of the cab. Her hair was seductively brushing against his neck and cheek, making him yearn for her.

Unbuckling his seat belt, Finn quickly got out of the driver's seat and rounded the hood of his truck to get to Connie's side.

She was fumbling with her belt when he opened her door.

She raised her head and he'd never seen her look so vulnerable. "It won't open," she complained.

Finn reached over and uncoupled the seat belt, freeing her. The second he did, she all but slid into him as she got off the seat and out of the truck.

Looking up into his face, she declared, "I give you permission."

"Permission?" he echoed. Very carefully, he made sure she could stand, then removed his hands from her waist. "Permission for what?"

She stepped in closer again, as if there was a magnetic charge between her body and his. "Permission to do something about wanting me."

Oh, God, if only... he caught himself thinking before he shut down his thoughts.

"Connie, you're a little tipsy. Maybe this isn't the right time," he began, desperately trying to do the right thing. But the ground beneath his feet was swiftly eroding.

"I know exactly what I'm saying," she corrected. "What I don't have the courage to say during regular hours."

Finn told himself not to listen, and he tried to get her to go into the trailer. Instead, she whirled around, made a funny little noise about how dizzy that made her feel. Then, before he knew what was happening, she had anchored her arms around his neck, pushed herself up as high as she could and before he could stop her, she'd managed to press her lips against his.

At first, it was just the excitement of making contact that zipped through him like static electricity. But as she pulled herself up a little higher and pressed her lips against his a little more forcefully, all sorts of tantalizing things began happening all through his body.

And not just his body, he realized a second later because the woman on the other side of her all-but-death grip was definitely responding to him. He could feel her body, soft and pliant, against his. Could feel her lips against his, no longer just a target, a passive receiver, but most definitely in the game.

All the way in the game.

Before he knew what was happening, he found himself responding to Connie. *Wanting* Connie with a level of desire that took him completely by surprise and totally threw him off his game.

He enfolded her in his arms, deepening the kiss she had begun even as it took him prisoner.

And then, as a sliver of common sense returned, pricking at his conscience, Finn forced himself to stop kissing her. Forced himself to put some distance, however minuscule, between them.

Taking hold of both her arms—to keep himself at bay as well as her—he gently pushed Connie back and said, "You don't want to do this."

There was a very strange light in her eyes, mixing in with the definite glimmer of mischief.

"Guess again," she said in a low, husky voice just before she retargeted his mouth again, sealing hers to it.

Finn knew damn well that he was supposed to be the sane one here, the one who was supposed to push her away again for her own good and keep pushing until she finally stopped coming at him. But he had used up his small supply of nobility quickly and she had refused to listen, refused to back away the way he'd told her to.

And damn, he'd been wanting this since the first time he'd turned around and saw her out there on the ranch, standing next to her less-than-useful sports car, looking at him as if she'd never seen a bare-chested man sweating in the hot sun before. She had generated a strong wave of desire within him then, and that wave had never really subsided, never receded so much as an iota.

Instead, it had remained suspended, waiting to be released.

Waiting for an opportunity like this.

Before he knew what he was doing and could discover a way to talk himself out of it, he swept Connie up into his arms. Then, pushing his shoulder against the trailer door to open it, Finn carried her inside.

The second the door was closed—and even before—Connie was all over him—marking his total undoing.

He could hardly keep up with her.

Her hands were everywhere, tugging at his clothing, skimming along his body, coaxing him to let go of his last thread of sanity and come to her.

And then he did.

He remembered the whole scenario taking place in what amounted to a hot haze, a frenzy of activity. A strange wildness had seized him as he found himself wanting her so very badly that it actually physically *hurt*. Wanting her and waiting for even an instant hurt in such a way that it felt as if it almost turned the air in his lungs to a solid substance.

She was going to regret this, a little voice in her head told her over and over, taunting her. Pointing out obvious things.

The actual deed couldn't possibly live up to the expectations she had built up in her head. She was just setting herself up for a fall.

And worst of all, he was going to brag about this to his friends, tell them that she was an easy mark and not really worth the effort in the end.

He'd disappoint her and she him.

All these things raced through her mind at top speed, repeating themselves over and over again. They should have stopped her.

On some level, she knew that.

But even so, her body was begging her not to listen to anything but its own rhythms, its own demands. All along, if she was being honest with herself, she had known that this man was going to be her downfall and yet she'd still hired him, still kept him around.

Still allowed his presence to fuel her dreams at night, when her guard was so woefully down.

She couldn't put a stop to it, couldn't rescue herself at the last moment because she discovered that every moment was just too delicious for her to voluntarily end.

She reveled in the way his lips felt against her skin, creating an excruciatingly wondrous moist trail of kisses that covered her breasts, went down to her belly and even farther than that, creating a dizzying warmth at the very core of her.

A warmth that coupled with a fire, which reduced her to a mass of rejoicing whimpers as climaxes blossomed within her over and over again.

Encased in dusky desire, Connie uttered not a single murmur of protest as she heard rather than saw Finn sweep away the schedules she'd labored so hard over, sending them all tumbling to the floor as he cleared the drawing board for her.

For them.

Squeals of ecstasy escaped her as he pushed her down onto the cleared flat surface and proceeded to make love to every inch of her, using his hands, his lips, his very breath to claim each part of her as his very own.

And when restraint tore at the weakened ties that were meant to keep her in place, when she arched and bucked against his body, silently begging for the union it'd promised, he gave in and took her, capturing her mouth at the last second so that they were joined together at all possible points.

The eternal dance began, and it was one that, to her stunned delight, Connie quickly mastered, getting in sync with each of his movements so that only a moment into the dance, they began to move as one, increasing the tempo as one.

And reaching the highest peak of pleasure as one, as well.

She felt the rainbow reach out and claim her, filling her with such exquisite euphoria that she didn't want to ever let it go.

This was where true happiness had been hiding from her all along.

And he had brought it to her.

Chapter Fourteen

Sanity returned far too swiftly.

It wore spurs on its boots and tracked a layer of mud all over Finn's conscience. The weight of his conscience was almost too oppressive to bear.

Pivoting on his elbows, Finn did his best to create space between their bodies, then moved over to one side, separating from her completely. He didn't know whether to apologize to her for what had happened, or just allow the silence to grow until it filled the room and overtook them, leaving no opening for conversation.

Rather than turn from him the way he expected her to, Connie just watched him. If she'd been giddy and tipsy before, she appeared to be totally clear-eyed now.

Was she angry? Did she think he took advantage of the situation and of her?

Did she hate him for it?

The silence continued to grow, becoming unwieldy to the point that he felt he just couldn't tolerate it any longer. Silence had never bothered him before, but it did now.

"Say something," Finn finally urged. But even as he was on the verge of begging her to speak, he braced himself for what he felt was inevitably coming: a barrage of words that would most likely compare him to the very lowest life form on the face of the earth.

What he found he wasn't prepared for was the actual word that did leave her lips.

"Wow."

Finn blinked, utterly positive that he had misheard her. Almost hesitantly, he whispered in confusion, "Say again?"

"Wow," she repeated, this time accompanying the word with a breathy sigh. "You know, I think the earth actually moved." She turned into him to see his face more clearly. "You don't have earthquakes down in this part of Texas, do you?"

"No," he replied uncertainly, studying her. Was she pulling his leg? Getting him to lower his guard before she hit him with a lethal punch?

"Didn't think so," she said, the smile taking on a dreamy quality. "Then I guess *wow* stands."

Her reaction just wasn't sinking in. He was still waiting for an explosion. "You're not angry?" Finn asked, still more than a little uncertain as he studied her demeanor.

"No, why would you think that I was angry?" She sat up for the first time. "Do I look angry?" Connie asked, glancing around to see if there was some sort of a reflecting surface available to her. She wanted to see herself so she could ascertain whether or not *she* thought she looked angry.

"No, you don't," he told her, treading very lightly. "But I thought...well... I thought that you'd feel I took advantage of you, and also you're my boss."

So that was it, Connie thought. At that moment, Finn went up another notch in her estimation. He really *was* a good guy.

"I had one drink," Connie admitted. "Not so much that I can't remember that I was the one who made the first moves—" she pointed out. "I kissed you first, not the other way around."

"So you're not angry," he concluded, wanting to be absolutely sure.

"Right now I'm still too tingly to be angry," Connie freely admitted—another first for her, she thought. She'd made love before, but each time all her feelings, all her reactions, were neatly compartmentalized. This deliriously happy feeling was definitely something new—and it thrilled her. Probably more than it should, she realized. But she just couldn't get herself to put a lid on it. So, just for tonight, she allowed herself to enjoy it.

Connie glanced down on the floor at the flurry of papers scattered there. "I will, however, be upset in the morning when I try to put all those schedules into some kind of order again."

That *had* been his fault. He'd swept her schedules to the floor. "I can help with that," Finn quickly volunteered.

"How?" Connie asked with a laugh. "By sweeping them out of the trailer?" she asked, amusement playing on her lips.

"By organizing them for you on my own time," he told her, sitting up beside her and looking at the mess below their feet. He was acutely aware of her sitting like that beside him. "But right now, if you're sure you're not angry…"

She turned her face to his and softly whispered, "Yes?"

He'd just had her and here he was wanting her again. Wanting her so badly, he felt himself literally *aching* for her. "I'd like to make love to you properly."

She pretended to look at him with wide-eyed confusion. "Oh, then what we just did, that was improper?"

He was fairly certain there were several states where what they'd just done would have been banned. "Highly."

"I see," she murmured thoughtfully. "And now you'd like to show me how it should have actually been done, is that it?"

His smile reached out to all parts of him, shining in his eyes as well as on his lips and in his demeanor. "Yes, I would."

Connie slid off the drawing board, her bare feet touching the scattered papers on the floor. She nodded her head slowly, as if she was thinking it over. "Never let it be said that I refused to leave myself open to a learning experience."

Finn followed suit, standing up beside her.

It was all she needed. Connie wound her arms around his neck, vividly aware of the fact that they were both still very nude.

She smiled up into his eyes. "You do realize that I'm still just a little dazed."

His arms went around her, bringing her even closer to him than a sigh. "I'm counting on it." When he saw her raise an eyebrow at his statement, Finn was quick to explain, "You're a lot less inhibited—and a great deal more trusting."

She saw no reason to argue that. He was right. "I'll have to work on that. Tomorrow," she decided. "I'll work on it tomorrow."

Because tonight, she knew she would be otherwise occupied.

And thrilled because of it.

Finn approached her carefully a little after eight the next morning, not quite sure what to expect or how to behave. He'd slipped out quietly from her trailer an hour before dawn. He'd wanted to give Connie her privacy, and he wasn't sure just how she would deal with the sight of him in her bed now that they had to go back to work.

If there was shame and discomfort on her part, since he was the cause of it, he wanted to spare her the sight of him for as long as possible.

At the same time, he knew he didn't have the luxury of simply going into hiding. He was her foreman, her second in command and as such, he had to be there, available for her *to* command.

Approaching her trailer, he knocked lightly, gave himself to the count of three, braced his shoulders and then walked in, every part of him prepared for some form of rejection, denouncement or whatever it was that would make Connie feel vindicated.

Finn was far too much of a realist to believe that fairy tales went on forever. He was just hoping that she didn't ultimately hate him for last night because for him, last night would live on in the annals of his mind for a very, very long time.

When she heard the door opening, Connie glanced over her shoulder. "Morning. I was beginning to think you were going to sleep in today."

Connie waved her hand, indicating the tall, covered white container on the side of her drawing board. An opened, partially empty container was standing right next to it.

"Got you some black coffee at Miss Joan's,"

she went on, turning back to her work. "The woman is selling India ink as coffee, but she swears that it gets your motor running, so drink up. We've got a really full day ahead of us if we've got a prayer of keeping this puppy on schedule."

Though he'd always thought of himself as being able to roll with punches, Finn was having trouble processing what was going on. Not because he was hungover, but because Connie seemed so different, so much— *looser,* for lack of a better word—than she had been before. And definitely more upbeat and cheerful. She still looked like the same woman, the same beautiful blue eyes, the same killer figure, but it was as if she was a newer, more improved version of herself. If she'd been a software program, he would have thought of her as Connie 2.0. He stared at the covered, oversize paper container she'd pointed to on the drawing board. "You got me coffee?" That alone was enough to throw him for a loop.

She nodded again. "Just in case you were having trouble getting in gear this morning."

"You have any of this?" he asked.

"I don't drink India ink," she informed him matter-of-factly. "I did get myself a cup of regular coffee, though. Just enough coffee to give the creamer something to work with and lighten," she told Finn. Now that he looked into her container, he could see that the contents appeared to be exceedingly light, close to the color of milk itself. "Now drink up, Finn," she was saying, "we're wasting daylight."

That was an exaggeration. "It isn't even eight yet," he pointed out.

But Connie absently nodded, as if he'd just agreed with her. "Like I said, we're wasting daylight."

Shaking his head even as humor crept in and curved the corners of his mouth, Finn took the lid off his container and took a very long, savory drag of his very black coffee.

As hoped for, the caffeine hit him with the kick of a disgruntled mule.

From that day forward, work continued at an almost effortless pace. There were a few hitches, and one on-site near accident with a girder, but overall, they kept on track, and the hotel took on its desired shape.

As it transformed from a hole in the ground to an edifice of impressive lines and structure, the citizens of Forever began to redesign their paths so that it took them by the excavation site. They came to note the progress or simply to watch some of their own operate the sophisticated machinery with precision.

They came to watch girders, posts, bolts and nails become something greater than the sum of their initial parts.

And a number of them, mostly the younger females, came to observe bare-chested men sweat and strain as they diligently created something they would all be proud of.

As Connie oversaw each and everyone's progress as they approached the end goal, occasionally issuing orders, or changing directives, her project, the bet she had with her father, turned into something far more meaningful to her. It no longer represented just winning an impulsive bet.

She was no longer the girl who was trying everything she could to get just a drop of her father's praise. There was far more going on here now.

The hotel became not only *her* project, but the crew working on its completion also became *her* men. And, she was delighted to discover, she was proud of them—proud of each and every one of them because of what they contributed to the whole.

And she fervently hoped that they returned the feeling, at least to some degree.

Somewhere along the line, shortly after Brett's engagement party—and her awakening as a woman—Connie began to document the crew's progress with the hotel. She would aim her smartphone at anything she felt should be preserved. This was her very first solo project and as such, like a first-born, each tiny milestone deserved to be forever frozen in time.

What she felt were the best shots she passed on, not to her father, but to Emerson, trusting him to choose which photo her father should see and which he might have found some minor, underlying fault with. It was a given fact that Calvin Carmichael was not known for his tact or restraint, especially where the company logo was involved. Emerson knew her father the way no other living soul did, and she trusted him to make the proper judgment calls on her behalf.

She could also trust him to be on her side. True to his nature, Emerson would send back an encouraging text that praised not just her efforts, but also her progress and the way the hotel was obviously shaping up. He was her own personal cheering section, and Connie loved him for it the way she knew she could never hope to love her father. On the home front, her life was also progressing equally well.

What could have become a very awkward situation between her and Finn—with neither of them knowing how to behave or react to one another—became, in fact, a very comfortable existence that they found themselves falling into without any actual discussion on their parts. Certainly no attempts to lay down any groundwork for themselves.

Connie was a woman who had, from a very young age, lived by her schedules. She always had to have her days mapped out from moment one to way beyond the final time frame. It made her feel as if she had control. And yet this sort of spontaneous forward movement worked for her. Not knowing worked for her. As did the delicious warmth of anticipation. And holding her breath when Finn walked up behind her, waiting for the first moment that his hand would brush against her shoulder, or touch her face.

Or the first moment that he would make her insane with desire.

They made love every night, the perfect ending to a perfect day. She had never been happier—as long as she didn't allow herself to dwell even fleetingly on the specter looming in the background: the completion of her project.

For now, she just took heart in the fact that the project was progressing well ahead of schedule and she, well, she was progressing in directions she had never dreamed she would.

As the days and weeks went by, Connie began to think of Forever as her special magical place, except that she knew Forever was real, too.

Still, because it had become so very special, she fervently hoped that Forever—and Finn—wouldn't disappear.

"What's that you're humming?" Finn asked her as they stood off to the side one day, observing the day's progress.

"I didn't realize I was humming," she confessed. "Just some nameless tune to keep my spirits up."

She didn't want to admit that what was actually keeping her spirits up was the fact that he was at her side from morning to night— and thereafter.

Work-wise, there had been a problem with the design when it came to the plumbing on

the ground floor, but she had managed to resolve it with a few key strokes of her pen on
the blueprints, then conveyed what needed
to be done by way of integral changes to the
men installing the pipes.

All of which had left Finn in complete
awe of her—and also drove home the stark
realization—again—that she didn't belong
here. It was further proof to him that once
this hotel, which was so very important to
her, was finally finished, Connie would go
back to her upscale world and be permanently
gone from his life.

Which, had this been any one of a number
of other times in his life—involving other
women—would have been fine with him.

But it wasn't fine this time.

Because this wasn't like any of those other
times. This time, he admitted to himself, was
different because *she* was different.

And he was different because of that.

Different because he was in love with her.

It had hit him one night as they were making
love in her bed. Hit him with all the subtlety
of a rampaging mustang trying to divest itself
of a newly cinched saddle. He felt a tenderness
toward her, a sensation he hadn't experienced

before, a desire to protect her not just for a little while, but for all the years to come.

That part had become clear to him when he discovered his desire to shield Connie from her father's harsh behavior. Something had been bothering her for the past few hours. He was aware of it even as they were making love.

"What's wrong?" he asked her as they lay there together, the sounds of heavy breathing mingling and fading.

"Nothing."

"I know you. That's not *nothing*. Now out with it—or do I have to torture you to get it out of you?" As if to make good on his threat, he wiggled his fingers before her as if he was about to tickle her. The second he brushed his fingers against her, Connie quickly surrendered.

"It's nothing, really. I sent my father a text update, complete with photos and the fact that we were way ahead of schedule."

"Did he respond?"

"Oh, he responded all right. He texted back 'Stop bragging. It's not finished yet. You could still fail.'" Connie shrugged. "I suppose it's just the way he is, and I shouldn't have expected any other response from him.

It's just that every once in a while, I keep hoping he'd change. That this one time, he'd tell me he was satisfied."

"And that he was proud of you?" Finn guessed.

"Yeah, there's that, too," Connie admitted with a shrug.

Finn could feel anger building up. Anger aimed at a man who had no idea how lucky he was to have a daughter like Connie. "Leopards don't change their spots," he told her gently.

A smile played on her lips. She knew he was trying his best to cheer her up, to make her focus on what she had and not feel inadequate because of what she'd failed to achieve.

"Very profound."

"Also very true," he pointed out.

She sighed and nodded. Finn was doing his best, and she was grateful to him for it. "My father doesn't matter."

"Damn straight he doesn't matter," he'd told her, surprising her with the fierceness in his voice because up until now, Finn hadn't really commented on her father at all. "He's never going to be satisfied and even if he thinks you've done better than fantastic, he's not about to tell you because somehow, he

feels that would be cutting down *his* image."
His eyes held hers as he tried to make her
understand what seemed so obvious to him.
"Connie, you could do the best damn job in
the whole world, and that man isn't going to
tell you. He's just going to look for something,
anything, to point to and find it lacking." He
raised her chin with the crook of his finger
when she tried to look away. "But you and I
know the truth."

"And what's the truth?" she asked with a
glimmer of a smile forming on her lips.

"That no one holds a candle to you. That
you've got a crew that'll follow any order you
give them not because it's an order but because you were the one who gave it. They're
not just a crew, Connie, they're *your* crew. I
know these guys. Trust me when I tell you
that really has to count for something," he
told her.

The smile that rose to her lips told him
that, at least for tonight, he'd gotten his point
across.

Chapter Fifteen

When her cell phone rang the following morning, Connie was busy finalizing the next week's schedule, which was, happily, far ahead of her original schedule. Things were moving right along, and she was exceedingly pleased with herself and with life in general.

She couldn't remember a time when she was happier—or even just as happy—than she was right now.

Pulling the phone out of her pocket, she pressed Accept without looking at the caller ID. Emerson called her almost daily to find out how things were going, and it was his voice she expected to hear on the other end when she said, "Hello."

But it wasn't Emerson.

It was her father.

Carmichael began without exchanging any pleasantries or even offering a perfunctory greeting. As always, he was all business. "I went over your latest report last night."

When he paused, she knew better than to press him for his opinion. It would come soon enough.

She was right. "I must say, you didn't mess up as badly as I expected you to."

Could she have expected anything more? Connie asked herself wearily. "Heady praise, Dad."

"I'm not in the business of heady praise," he told her curtly. "In case you've forgotten, I'm in the construction business. Which leads me to my next point. I've got a new project for you to supervise—it's a museum. Right up your alley. It's on the east coast so I'm pulling you off the hotel."

She felt as if she'd just walked across a land mine and it had gone off. "But the hotel's not finished," she protested.

"I'm not blind. I can see that," he snapped. "I'll be sending Tyler Anderson to oversee its completion. It's not your concern anymore, Constance. Pack. I want you here by morning."

"But—" She heard a strange noise on the other end of the line and found herself talking to dead air. Her father had terminated the call.

Frustration flared through her. "Damn," Connie muttered to herself as she continued to stare at the now silent phone in her hand.

There was a quick knock on her trailer door and the next moment, Finn stuck his head in. "Hey, we're sending out lunch orders to Miss Joan's, and I just wanted to ask what you wanted to eat today."

That was when he saw the shell-shocked expression on Connie's face. Lunch was forgotten. Finn came all the way into the trailer and crossed to her.

"What's wrong?" he asked.

And then he noticed the cell phone in her hand. His mind scrambled to put the pieces together. Had she just gotten bad news? Was that what was responsible for that completely devastated look on her face?

"What happened?" he prodded again. "Did your father just call?" She raised her eyes to his but still wasn't saying anything. "Talk to me, Connie. I can't help if you don't talk to me."

"You can't help even if I do," she answered quietly, staring unseeingly straight ahead of her. She felt as if everything was crumbling within her.

Taking hold of Connie's shoulders, he gently guided her to a chair and forced her to sit down.

"It was your father, wasn't it?" It was no longer a guess. Only her father could make her look like that. After a moment, Connie nodded. "What did he say? Because no matter what that man said, you know you're doing a damn good job here and—"

Her quiet voice cut through his loud one. "He wants me to come home."

Finn tried to make sense out of what she had just said. "When you finish?"

Connie slowly moved her head from side to side. "No, now."

That didn't make *any* sense. From what she'd told him, her father was obsessive about projects being completed on time, under budget and to reflect everyone's best work to date.

"But the hotel's not finished. You still—"

Connie turned to look at him, focusing on his face for the first time. She was struggling very hard not to cry.

"He's sending someone else to finish overseeing the job. He says he has another project for me. Seems there's a museum going up on the east coast he wants me to be involved in."

"The east coast?" Finn echoed. That was half a continent away. *She'd* be half a continent away, he thought, something twisting in his gut.

"The east coast," she repeated numbly.

"Are you going?" he asked, doing his best to suppress his anger at this unexpected, sudden blow.

Connie released a huge sigh that felt to her as if it went on forever. "He's my boss. I have to."

Finn wanted to argue that, but he knew he had no right. All he could do was ask questions. "Did he say why he wanted you off this project?"

Connie shook her head. "He's the boss. He doesn't have to explain anything. He never has before."

Finn told himself that his feelings about this unexpected turn of events, his feelings about her, didn't matter. That he'd known all along that this day was coming. It had just arrived a little sooner than he'd anticipated.

The important thing here was Connie. This

was what she'd wanted all along, to have her father recognize her ability to helm projects. The man clearly wouldn't be sending her to begin another one if he didn't feel that she was good when it came to setting things up and getting them rolling.

"How soon?" he asked her, the words tasting bitter in his mouth.

Her eyes shifted to his. "Soon" was all she said in reply. She couldn't bring herself to say "immediately" just yet. She knew that she would break down if she did.

"Well," Finn began, doing his best to sound philosophical and supportive instead of angry and exasperated, "this is what you've been hoping for all along, right?"

"Right," she answered without even attempting to sound enthusiastic.

She slanted a glance at Finn. Why wasn't he as upset about this as she was? Did he actually *want* her to go? Didn't he care that she wasn't staying?

Finn was doing his best to find his way through this emotional maze he suddenly found himself in. "In his own way, I guess your father's telling you that he thinks you're capable of representing him, of helming an important project. He's not asking you to accompany him but to go to the location without him. This means that he's admitting that you *can* fly solo," he said with as much enthusiasm as he could summon—all for her sake. But then he looked at her closely. "You're not smiling."

"Sure I am," she responded evasively. "On the inside."

"Oh. Sorry, I left my X-ray-vision glasses in my other jeans," he told her sarcastically. The next moment, he told himself that wasn't going to get him anywhere. He ditched the attitude. "So how much time *do* you have?" he asked, acutely aware of the minutes that were slipping away, out of his grasp. Quite possibly his last minutes with her.

"He wants me to be in Houston in the morning. That means I have to leave by tonight at the latest."

She was saying the words, but they still hadn't sunk in yet. She was leaving. Leaving Forever. Leaving crews who weren't just crews anymore; they had become her friends. Leaving a man who had her heart in his pocket.

"Tonight?" Finn questioned, his voice echoing in his own head. "He really does want you back immediately, doesn't he?"

Don't cry. Don't cry, she kept telling herself over and over again. "Looks that way."

"And he didn't give you a reason for all this hurry?" Finn pressed. He really *hated* things that didn't make any sense.

"I already told you," she said, bone-weary, "he's the boss. He doesn't have to explain himself or give reasons. He just gives orders."

Connie kept looking at him, silently begging Finn to tell her not to go. To come up with some lame excuse why she just couldn't pick up and leave right now. *Any* excuse.

But there was only silence in the trailer.

"The men aren't going to be happy," Finn finally said, speaking up.

"They need the money," she reminded him. That was what he'd told her at the outset of the job, that most of the people being hired were taking this on as an extra job. "They'll adjust."

Finn snorted. "Not readily."

"But eventually," Connie countered sadly.

She knew she was right. Within a few months, nobody would even remember that she had been here, Connie thought sadly. She felt as if someone had dropped an anvil on her chest. The upshot was that she was having trouble catching her breath as well as organizing her thoughts into a coherent whole.

Most of all, she was trying to deal with the realization that Finn seemed to be all right with the thought of her leaving. He hadn't said a word of protest, just asked her a few questions about the situation, that's all.

Well, what did you expect? That he'd fall down on one knee and beg you to stay? That he'd ask you to marry him because he just couldn't live a day without you? Get real, Con. This was a nice little interlude as far as he's concerned, but now it's over and it's time for him to move on. You move on, too. Move on, or become a laughingstock.

Connie raised her head and glanced in his direction. "If you don't mind, I've got a lot of things to do before I can leave, and I can do it faster if I'm by myself."

"Sure," he told her. "I'll get out of your hair" were his parting words as he left.

Connie nodded numbly in response.

But how do I get you out of my soul? she asked him silently, staring at the closed door.

With no need for restraint any longer, she allowed her tears to fall.

"Hey, what the hell happened to you?" Brett asked when Finn walked into the saloon a few minutes later.

Murphy's didn't officially open for another few hours although the doors weren't locked and even if they were, all three of the brothers had keys to the establishment since it belonged to all of them.

"You look like you just lost your best friend," Brett said, concerned when Finn didn't answer him.

Finn shrugged his shoulders, leaving his brother's question unanswered. Instead, he went behind the bar, took out a shot glass and then grabbed the first bottle of hard liquor within reach.

When he went to pour, Brett pushed the shot glass away. The alcohol wound up spilling onto the bar.

"I can always pour another shot," Finn said.

"And it'll land on the bar, same as the first shot," Brett informed him, "so unless you plan to lick yourself into a drunken stupor, put down the bottle and tell me what's going on with you."

"Always the big brother," Finn said sarcastically.

"Yeah, I am, so deal with it. Now what the hell's going on with you? You're not going anywhere until you tell me," Brett declared with finality.

Finn's throat felt incredibly dry as he said, "She's leaving."

"When the hotel is finished," Brett said, reviewing the facts as he knew them.

Finn's expression darkened further. "No, now. Today," he snapped. The hotel had a ways to go before it was completed. He still felt that Connie's abruptly leaving for a new project didn't make any sense. Though, he could admit he was more invested than he'd thought.

"Why? Did you two have a fight?"

"No, we didn't 'have a fight,'" Finn retorted angrily. "Her father decided he wanted her working on something else."

"What does Connie say about it?" Brett asked him quietly.

Finn blew out a shaky breath, angrier than he could ever remember being. "She isn't saying anything about it. She's going."

Brett continued to study his brother as he responded. "Did you ask her not to?"

"No," Finn bit off. It wasn't up to him to ask. It was up to her to *want* to stay, he thought, totally frustrated.

Brett gave up standing quietly on the sidelines. "Why the hell not?"

"What am I supposed to say?" Finn demanded.

"How about 'Connie, don't go. I love you.' From where I stand, that sounds pretty simple to me," Brett told him.

Didn't Brett understand what was at stake here? "I'd be asking her to give up everything, that big house, the future she's been working toward all these years. Give it all up and stay here in Forever with me." The inequality of that was staggering, Finn thought.

Brett nodded his head. "Sounds about right."

"Damn it, Brett. I haven't got anything to offer her," Finn cried angrily.

Brett looked at him for a long, long moment. And then he shook his head sadly. "If you think that, then you're dumber than I thought you were."

Finn gritted his teeth and ground out, "You're not helping."

"You're not listening," Brett countered. "Connie grew up in pretty much the lap of luxury from what she said—and she didn't seem able to crack a smile when she first got here. After working in Forever—and associating with your sorry ass—she's a completely different person. She looks *happy*.

That's what you can do for her. You can make her happy," Brett emphasized. "That's not as common a gift as you might think."

Finn waved a hand at his brother. Brett was giving him platitudes. "You don't know what you're talking about."

"Ask her to stay," Brett urged. "Honestly, what have you got to lose?"

"Face," Finn retorted. "If she turns me down, I can lose face."

Brett raised and lowered his shoulders in a careless, dismissive shrug. "It's not such a great face. No big loss. Might even be an improvement," he told Finn, keeping a straight face. And then he turned serious. "And if you don't ask her to stay, you'll never know if she would have."

Finn shook his head, rejecting the suggestion. "If she wanted to stay, she would."

Brett threaded his arm around his brother's shoulders. "Women operate under a whole different set of guidelines than we do, Finn. You should know that by now." Brett suddenly pushed his brother toward the front door. "Now stop being such a stubborn jerk and go tell her you want her to stay. That you *need* her to stay."

"It's not going to work," Finn insisted.

Brett pretended to consider that outcome. "Then you'll have the satisfaction of proving me wrong for the first time in your life."

Finn opened his mouth to argue that rather unenlightened assessment, then decided he didn't want to stay here, going round and round about a subject he felt neither one of them could successfully resolve.

Instead, he shoved the bottle he'd pulled from the shelf earlier back on the bar and stormed out of the saloon.

"Make me proud!" Brett called after him.

He didn't knock this time. Instead, Finn burst into the trailer, swinging the door open so hard that it hit the opposite side, making a resounding noise.

In the middle of packing, Connie jumped and swung around. "Finn, you scared the hell out of me," she cried, her hand covering her heart, which was pounding hard for more than one reason. Hope began to infuse itself through her—hope that maybe, just maybe happily-ever-after wasn't completely off the table. A hint of a smile broke through even as she held her breath.

And prayed that he would say something she needed to hear.

"Well, then we're even," he replied. "Because the thought of you leaving Forever is scaring the hell out of me."

She let the shirt she'd been folding drop from her hand as she regarded him. Just what was he up to? "You certainly didn't act like it did." It was an accusation more than an observation.

"No, I didn't," he agreed. The temper he'd been grappling with since he'd left her trailer was only beginning to come under control. "And you used the right word—act. I was *acting* like it didn't bother me because I knew that was what you'd wanted since you got here, to show your father that you could handle a project on your own, to show him that you were damn good for the company and deserved to be treated with respect instead of being treated like a lackey.

"And I knew that once you were finished building the hotel, you'd leave. I figured I was okay with that. But just now I had to *act* as if I was—because I wasn't. I wasn't *okay* with that. I wasn't *okay* with you leaving."

"You weren't?"

"No, I wasn't. And I'm not," he told her, changing his tenses to make her understand that his feelings were still ongoing. "Look, I know I don't have the right to ask you to stay, and I don't have anything that's close to measuring up to what you have waiting for you back in Houston. I don't even—"

Connie cut him off. "Ask me to stay," she said softly.

Finn was desperately searching for the right words to convince her to stay. When she interrupted, his train of thought came to a screeching halt. He *couldn't* have heard her right.

"What?"

"Ask me to stay," Connie repeated. "Say the word."

He stared at her in disbelief for a long moment, stunned into silence.

"Stay," he whispered quietly, certain that she was seeing how far she could get him to go. He honestly didn't know his limits right now.

And then he thought he was dreaming when he saw the smile that blossomed on her lips. It almost blinded him with its brilliance.

Connie stood on her tiptoes as she reached up and wrapped her arms around his neck.

"Okay," she replied, the word all but ringing with immeasurable joy.

"You're serious?" he asked.

Her eyes never left his. "I am if you are," she answered.

He hadn't known that a person could be this excited and happy while struggling with shock, all at the very same time.

"I love you," he told her. "You know that, right?"

He could have sworn that her eyes were laughing. "I do now."

"Don't you have anything you want to say to me?" he prodded. He'd laid himself on the line here, opened up his heart to her—and she hadn't told him how she felt about him. He held his breath, hoping that it wasn't all going to blow up on him.

"Kiss me, stupid," Connie responded, doing her best not to laugh.

He tried again. "Don't you have anything to say to me besides that?"

The smile slid over her lips by degrees, widening a little more every second. "Oh, yeah, right." And then she said in the most serious voice she could summon, "I love you, too."

"*Now* I'm going to kiss you stupid," he vowed. "As well as senseless."

She was ready and willing to have him try. All in all, it sounded like a lovely way to go.

"You have your work cut out for you," Connie warned him.

Finn's arms tightened around her a little more, bringing their bodies even closer together. "I sure hope so," he told her.

And he was prepared to love every second of it.

Epilogue

"And you're sure you're up to this?" Brett asked Liam for what seemed like the umpteenth time since yesterday morning when the wedding was given the green light by all concerned.

Standing beside him, Finn and Liam exchanged looks. In their joint recollection, they couldn't remember *ever* seeing their older brother look anywhere so nervous and unsettled. But then, Brett had never been in this sort of a situation before, either.

Brett and Alisha's wedding ceremony was only moments away from unfolding. Because of the extensive guest list—everyone wanted to attend—the couple was getting married in an outdoor ceremony performed at the ranch Brett had inherited.

Everything, including Liam's band, which was providing the music, had been set up outside. A canopy was put up to protect the food just in case the weather decided to reverse itself and go from the predicted sunny to rainy at the last moment.

Right now, the sun was shining, but Brett scarcely noticed. His attention was otherwise occupied by the thousand and one details that apparently went into planning a wedding. Brett was concerning himself needlessly inasmuch as his brothers, especially Finn, had for the most part taken over making all the arrangements.

But, as the oldest, Brett found he had trouble relinquishing control and just sitting back. He had just too much riding on all this.

"It's the 'Wedding March,'" Liam reminded his older brother. "I think I can handle the 'Wedding March,'" he said.

But Brett had to make sure. Liam was impulsive at times. "You're not going to suddenly decide to jazz it up or put in a beat, right?"

"What the 'Wedding March' needs is to have you calm down, big brother," Liam told him. "Just concentrate on remembering your vows and getting through the ceremony. I'll handle the music, okay?" he asked, flashing a sympathetic smile.

Brett blew out a breath, doing his best to get this unexpected case of nerves under control. "Okay."

"All you have to do is keep it together until the minister pronounces you husband and wife. After that, you're home free," Finn counseled.

"No, Finn. You've got that wrong. He's getting married. He's never going to be free again," Liam deadpanned affectionately.

That was enough to make Brett rally. "You two should be so lucky," he told them.

"Not me. I've got a lot of wild oats to sow yet," Liam informed his brother happily. Glancing at his watch, he announced, "Time to begin. Last chance to do something stupid and run," he said to Brett.

"Not a chance," Brett replied. Squaring his shoulders, he went to stand at his designated spot at the front of the newly constructed altar.

As his best man, Finn stood beside him—and thoughtfully watched the proceedings unfold.

* * *

"This has to be the most beautiful ceremony I've ever attended," Connie told Finn as they were dancing at the reception. "And I've been to more than my share," she confided.

At times it seemed like three quarters of her graduating class had all gotten married in recent years. Because of that, she found that it gave her less and less in common with people who used to be her friends. Their priorities slowly changed while hers had remained the same.

Until now.

"It's incredible," she went on to say, "considering that it seemed as if the whole town pitched in." In her book, that should have yielded a hodgepodge. Except that it didn't.

"They pretty much did—which is maybe *why* it turned out so well," Finn speculated. He knew the world she came from involved wedding planners, something that was completely foreign to his way of thinking. "Wedding planners don't have a personal stake in things turning out well, just a professional one. It keeps them removed."

"Bartender, master builder, wedding organizer. I guess there's just no end to your talents," Connie teased even though she was only half kidding. "A regular Renaissance man, that's you," she told the man who filled her days and her dreams, as well.

"I don't know about that Renaissance part, but I am a regular man," Finn replied.

Not so regular, Connie thought happily. As far as she was concerned, the word for Finn was *extraordinary.* Each day she felt as if she loved him a little more. Now that she had made the bold move of detaching herself from her father's company—with the stipulation that she be allowed to finish the hotel she'd started—she had half expected Finn to back away from her. After all, she wasn't that rich woman she'd been just a short while ago, just a woman who was still determined to make her mark on the world—but for a whole different reason.

But instead of backing away, Finn had been incredibly supportive, telling her she was doing the right thing, especially when she told him that she wanted to form her own construction company and take on projects that would help improve the community where she chose to do her work.

The first place she intended to start was on the reservation. The buildings there were in desperate need of repair or rebuilding from scratch. She had enough in her trust fund, left to her by her maternal grandfather, to help her with her goals for a very long time to come.

"How do you feel about marrying a regular guy?" he asked her out of the blue, just after twirling her around as the music went from a slow dance to one with a pulsating beat.

It took her a moment to regain her balance. "Depends on who the regular guy is," she said guardedly. She hung on to her imagination, refusing to allow it to run away with her.

"Me, Connie. Me."

She stopped dancing and stared at Finn, completely stunned. Had she really heard him correctly? "You're asking me to marry you?"

"That's the general gist of this conversation, yes," he acknowledged. "Move your feet, Connie," he coaxed gently. "You're attracting attention."

She did as he asked, hardly aware of moving at all. "Really?"

"Well, you probably always attract attention, looking the way you do, but—"

"No, I'm not asking if I'm attracting attention," she said impatiently. "I'm asking if you're really asking me to marry you. Are you?"

His mouth suddenly felt dry and just like

that, he completely understood why Brett had been so nervous earlier. One way or another, this was going to be life-altering for him. If Connie said no, he'd be crushed and if she said yes—well, she *had* to say yes, he told himself. He couldn't live with any other decision.

"With every fiber of my being," he answered her. Then, to further prove he was serious, Finn made it formal. "Constance Carmichael, will you do me the extreme honor of becoming my wife?"

"I don't know about the extreme honor part, but yes, I'll marry you," she told him as her eyes welled up with tears.

As for Finn, his eyes lit up. The next moment, he sealed their agreement with one of the longest kisses that the good citizens of Forever had ever witnessed.

One of Liam's band members, Sam, nudged him in the ribs and when he looked at Sam, the latter pointed toward the lip-locked couple.

Liam glanced over and then smiled. "Next," he murmured under his breath, because it was clearly indicated that Finn was next when it came to being altar-bound.

Liam knew he would be the last Murphy brother left standing alone.

The thought made him smile even more broadly.

* * * * *

HOME on the RANCH

YES! Please send me the **Home on the Ranch Collection** in Larger Print. This collection begins with 3 FREE books and 2 FREE gifts in the first shipment. Along with my 3 free books, I'll also get the next 4 books from the Home on the Ranch Collection, in LARGER PRINT, which I may either return and owe nothing, or keep for the low price of $5.24 U.S./ $5.89 CDN each plus $2.99 for shipping and handling per shipment*. If I decide to continue, about once a month for 8 months I'll get 6 or 7 more books, but will only need to pay for 4. That means 2 or 3 books in every shipment will be FREE! If I decide to keep the entire collection, I'll have paid for only 32 books because 19 books are FREE! I understand that accepting the 3 free books and gifts places me under no obligation to buy anything. I can always return a shipment and cancel at any time. My free books and gifts are mine to keep no matter what I decide.

268 HCN 3760 468 HCN 3760

Name   (PLEASE PRINT)

Address   Apt. #

City   State/Prov.   Zip/Postal Code

Signature (if under 18, a parent or guardian must sign)

Mail to the **Reader Service:**
IN U.S.A.: P.O. Box 1867, Buffalo, NY. 14240-1867
IN CANADA: P.O. Box 609, Fort Erie, Ontario L2A 5X3

HRCBPA18

Get 2 Free Books,
Plus 2 Free Gifts—
just for trying the Reader Service!

HARLEQUIN®
SPECIAL EDITION

Get 2 Free Books, Plus 2 Free Gifts –

just for trying the **Reader Service!**

YES! Please send me 2 FREE novels from the Essential Romance or Essential Suspense Collection and my 2 FREE gifts (gifts are worth about $10 retail). After receiving them, if I don't wish to receive any more books, I can return the shipping statement marked "cancel." If I don't cancel, I will receive 4 brand-new novels every month and be billed just $6.74 each in the U.S. or $7.24 each in Canada. That's a savings of at least 16% off the cover price. It's quite a bargain! Shipping and handling is just 50¢ per book in the U.S. and 75¢ per book in Canada*. I understand that accepting the 2 free books and gifts places me under no obligation to buy anything. I can always return a shipment and cancel at any time. The free books and gifts are mine to keep no matter what I decide.

Please check one: ☐ Essential Romance ☐ Essential Suspense
194/394 MDN GMWR 191/391 MDN GMWR

Name _____ (PLEASE PRINT)

Address _____ Apt. #

City _____ State/Prov. _____ Zip/Postal Code

Signature (if under 18, a parent or guardian must sign)

Mail to the **Reader Service:**
IN U.S.A.: P.O. Box 1341, Buffalo, NY 14240-8531
IN CANADA: P.O. Box 603, Fort Erie, Ontario L2A 5X3

Want to try two free books from another line?
Call 1-800-873-8635 or visit www.ReaderService.com.

*Terms and prices subject to change without notice. Prices do not include applicable taxes. Sales tax applicable in NY. Canadian residents will be charged applicable taxes. Offer not valid in Quebec. This offer is limited to one order per household. Books received may not be as shown. Not valid for current subscribers to the Essential Romance or Essential Suspense Collection. All orders subject to approval. Credit or debit balances in a customer's account(s) may be offset by any other outstanding balance owed by or to the customer. Please allow 4 to 6 weeks for delivery. Offer available while quantities last.

Your Privacy—The Reader Service is committed to protecting your privacy. Our Privacy Policy is available online at www.ReaderService.com or upon request from the Reader Service.

We make a portion of our mailing list available to reputable third parties that offer products we believe may interest you. If you prefer that we not exchange your name with third parties, or if you wish to clarify or modify your communication preferences, please visit us at www.ReaderService.com/consumerschoice or write to us at Reader Service Preference Service, P.O. Box 9062, Buffalo, NY 14240-9062. Include your complete name and address.

STRS17R2

Get 2 Free Books,
Plus 2 Free Gifts—
just for trying the Reader Service!

Get 2 Free Books,

Get 2 Free Books,
Plus 2 Free Gifts—
just for trying the Reader Service!

READERSERVICE.COM

Manage your account online!

- Review your order history
- Manage your payments
- Update your address

*We've designed the
Reader Service website
just for you.*

Enjoy all the features!

- Discover new series available to you, and read excerpts from any series.
- Respond to mailings and special monthly offers.
- Browse the Bonus Bucks catalog and online-only exculsives.
- Share your feedback.

Visit us at:

ReaderService.com